A Tiler's Afternoon

Lars Gustafsson

A Tiler's Afternoon

Translated by Tom Geddes

A NEW DIRECTIONS BOOK

Originally published as *En kakelsättares eftermiddag* by Bokförlaget Natur och Kultur, Stockholm, in 1991. This English translation is published by arrangement with Harvill, an imprint of HarperCollins*Publishers*, London.

The first four chapters of *A Tiler's Afternoon* appeared in *Fiction*.

Manufactured in the United States of America
New Directions Books are printed on acid-free paper.
First published as New Directions Paperbook 761 in 1993
Published simultaneously in Canada by Penguin Books Canada Limited

Library of Congress Cataloging-in-Publication Data

Gustafsson, Lars, 1936-
   [Kakelsättares eftermiddag. English]
   A tiler's afternoon / Lars Gustafsson.
      p.   cm. — (New Directions paperbook ; 761)
   ISBN 0-8112-1240-8 (pbk. alk. paper)
   I. Title.
PT9876.17.U8K2913   1993
839.7'374—dc20   93-16457
                                                  CIP

New Directions Books are published for James Laughlin
by New Direction Publishing Corporation,
80 Eighth Avenue, New York 10011

CONTENTS

"*L'histoire d'une vie, quelle qu'elle soit, est l'histoire d'un échec.*"

JEAN-PAUL SARTRE:
"*L'Etre et le Néant*"

Collected works

THERE WAS A MAN called Torsten Bergman, a thin man with white hair. He was a tiler, born in 1917. So on the grey November morning in 1982 when this story takes place, in Uppsala, Sweden, he was already 65 years old. He slept in a bed that had once been double and shared. Now it was single and its sheets rarely washed. Old newspapers and a few empty bottles lay strewn at random across the floor, and over in the corner was the old black mat covered in hairs where the dog slept.

The day began in the only way it could: the grass already touched by the first frost, the dog run off days ago, all life a mystery, his own most of all. The garden a mess, its cultivation neglected. The house was old, made of wood that had once been painted green, now dove-grey and peeling. Weary boughs of old and heavy apple trees hung threateningly across the rotting verandah. The entire garden a littered, jumbled monument to the collected works of his whole life. Or, as some might have put it, the failures.

The morning light, still grey and full of naked ice-cold drops from the night's rain, and clouded by indescribably grey and hazy dreams, was kept out to some extent by the heavy yellow blind at the window.

The garden, which to tell the truth wasn't much of a garden any more, had for the last fifteen years had a fence of corrugated iron instead of the old wooden one. When the newspaper boy banged his handlebars against it on his way to the neighbour's letter box between five and six in the morning, the sound travelled the whole length of the fence, like a clash of cymbals; he loathed this noise that reminded him every morning of the need to get up, to live again. How much wouldn't he rather have stayed in his dreams, among the grey and indistinct shadows!

He would have preferred so much more not to exist than to exist. If anyone had asked him what he thought.

It was in that room that the telephone rang, with a sharp and piercing trill, at half past six one Thursday morning in Uppsala in November 1982. It was the start of a Thursday without any real end. But no one could know that yet.

He had no desire to look out of the window. He knew only too well what there was outside.

The advantage of a fence, a solid fence, of corrugated iron, was that it didn't rot like the frail wooden palings that the dreamy turn-of-the-century architects had provided for these little workers' houses. It lasted well. At one time the houses had been intended for people employed at Ekeby factory. The factory wasn't there any more. But the fence was. It kept out thieves and small boys, and above all you could gather together within its protection all the things you wanted to hang on to. There was no need for flower-beds now, when you didn't have a wife.

An old plumber's bench, no fewer than three different wheelbarrows, a wooden motorboat that hadn't been out in the bay since the fifties when his wife Britta had departed this life. It had become something of a rock, one of the fixed components of the garden. It had lain covered in a tarpaulin since then, and was probably now no more than a hiding place for rats, and thus equally appreciated by the many fat and well-trained domestic cats of the neighbourhood. What else was there? A whole pile of cast-iron pipes that he'd once got in exchange for something else and that were meant for a pipe-replacement job that it was probably already too late for. Tiles, protected under sheets of fibreboard, timber that you'd been able to crumble between your fingers for ages, and right at the bottom a lawn-mower that had been bought and had its initial roll over the spring grass in 1947 when their son had been born.

At first he understood not a word the voice said on the telephone. He was finding it increasingly difficult to comprehend what was said to him on the telephone, especially in the mornings. And quite often at such moments he was tempted to slam down the receiver in anger when he couldn't really grasp who was speaking or what they wanted. Voices on the telephone seemed to take too much for granted. Only when he realised that the voice had a Finnish accent did it become intelligible.

There was nothing special about the man who was ringing. And nothing special about what he wanted, either. The voice belonged to a plumber, an electrician, a jack-of-all-trades, called Pentti. Torsten knew him quite well in a way. They'd worked together on masses of jobs once upon a time. The last one they'd done was laying a new kitchen floor for one of those firms that provided the food for airline passengers out at Stockholm airport.

That had been a disgusting job, but it had paid well. He'd hardly had a sober day for three weeks afterwards. He'd taken a taxi to the nearest liquor store to avoid being squashed in with the old women on the bus. For the last few years he'd come to dislike travelling by bus more and more; everything that forced him together with other people gave him a feeling of suffocating. Then he very easily got angry and aggressive.

The kitchen of the big airline was incredibly large, and there was a host of bustling, noisy and quite unintelligible little foreigners, or whatever the hell they were, who went on boiling and frying non-stop in one half of the room at huge restaurant stoves with the mechanical energy of tin men wound up with keys in their backs, while in the other half the old rubber matting was being ripped up and making clouds of dust and scattering shreds of old glue. The idea was that it should be replaced with tiles, and Torsten and Petterson from Gottsunda had got the job on a cash basis. Nowadays he only worked in the underground economy since he'd managed to get sickness benefit on account of his stomach. Petterson from Gottsunda had sworn never to do a legal job again after that bloody tax inspector had come down on him with a bill for unpaid tax of fifty thousand crowns in 1973, and he'd kept the vow honourably ever since. Unfortunately he'd disappeared from that job after a few days, leaving Torsten on his own. His heart had gone out of it. Not all that surprising in the circumstances.

Under that rubber matting there was a fermenting semi-organic mess – compost might be a better word – of food scraps and gravy spills or God knows what: remnants of all the food since the fifties that hadn't quite made it into the airline passengers' meals, now forming an unspeakably disgusting glue-like sludge. He'd had to shovel it out with a spade and wheelbarrow. It was pale-yellow like cat's piss, and gave off a stench that language hardly had words for. It was a mixture of old gravy and the smell of a fox farm, a urinal with putrid sour milk in it.

Never in his whole life had he been involved with anything so repulsively awful. Again and again he'd had to rush out

4

and be sick as a dog in the piles of snow outside the hangar-like kitchens. And all the time those Arabs, or whatever the devil those dark-skinned little people were, had continued frying on their disgusting great hot-plates and cooking in gigantic pots in that hell-hole of a kitchen, while the dust and the muck billowed around them. He'd got the worst of it out in the end and was able to spread the floor cement and lay his Finnish tiles. After that it didn't smell quite so appalling.

The next bloody problem was stopping those damned people from walking on the newly-laid tiles. It didn't seem to help however much he tried to talk to them. Perhaps they'd never seen tiles before. They were cracking and coming apart at the joins and moving all over the place. He wondered sometimes if tile cement and grouting had been quietly deteriorating in recent years without his really noticing.

It had become more and more difficult, God knows why, to get tiles to stay on the walls nowadays. Whether it was the fault of the walls or of the tiles wasn't easy to tell. It was a job like any other. There was nothing especially remarkable about it. Jobs were never particularly enjoyable. If you could get them done without paying tax and all that crap then there was at least some point in them. Otherwise there was no point at all.

But anyway Pentti, that plumber who could hardly speak Swedish, was a decent and helpful sort of fellow. When the cold sweats were at their worst and Torsten was throwing up again, Pentti had left his plumbing work, wrapped a wet towel round his nose and mouth, found another cement shovel and helped him to dig out the worst of the shit. The young guys who were driving the food trucks backwards and forwards to the waiting charter passengers had roared with laughter at them.

This time it wouldn't be such *fun*, said Pentti on the

telephone. It was tiles to be put up in a two-storey property that was being renovated. Bathrooms and laundry rooms.

It seemed that someone had started to renovate a big old-fashioned house. Two substantial flats with spacious bathrooms and laundry rooms, if Pentti was to be believed. Apparently there was someone still living in the unmodernised part on the upper floor. But they had to get out, and there was supposed to be something going on with the rent board. So it wasn't very clear when and how the whole thing would end. And on top of all that there'd evidently been some problem with the tilers.

They'd cleared off without any notice and left half-finished everything that they were supposed to have done on the basement level, the bathroom and washroom and sauna and laundry room in the cellar. Perhaps they'd found a better job elsewhere. Or perhaps they'd fallen out with the owner, or with each other. It was hard to tell. There were so many casual workers nowadays coming and going from one day to the next. In point of fact probably no one knew whether they were even tilers by trade, these men who'd disappeared.

They might have drunk themselves into a stupor, since they'd got the money for tile cement, floor cement and other materials, become so drunk that they couldn't hold their pliers, hammers or trowels any more. Or perhaps the explanation was that the owner was so bloody mean or difficult that it had been completely impossible to reason with him.

Pentti didn't know very much about him. But at least it was clear that these weren't the sort of people who take up a loan for an energy-saving installation from the government for 30,000 crowns, and then stick the boiler out in the garden to rust and go off to Majorca on the money instead. Pentti had seen that kind of thing before, even as close to home as his neighbour out in Graneberg where he lived.

6

Pentti was the type you might still come across, even in 1982, cutting fresh grass for his rabbits along the roadside verges in the spring evenings and taking it home in a sack on his carrier. He wasn't exactly stingy, but he had a certain knack of looking after himself. Pentti didn't approve of people who would use a government energy loan to go to Majorca.

There was no question of their being that sort. And the one thing Pentti was sure he could promise without any doubt was that there was also no question of their being the sort of people who demanded receipts and sent details of what they'd paid out to the authorities and the tax man. That went without saying. But who owned the building and who was going to move into the ground-floor flat before the end of November – well, that he didn't know. That was something Torsten would obviously have to find out for himself. And the same went for who would pay him. Pentti's view in general was that you shouldn't worry too much about the details in life. The main thing was to see the broad picture.

Pentti wouldn't be coming himself. Not this time. He was just a helping hand, so to speak, a go-between and an emergency number, all rolled into one. What had actually happened was that when there was trouble with the other tiler, there had been some sort of fuss about the plumber too. And Pentti had had to step in for him for a few days, mainly because the first plumber had got into trouble and been told off at his full-time council job because he was falling asleep more and more often during his working hours there. He had apparently worked on this damned house right into the night.

Breathing heavily, Torsten struggled and strained with a dreadful old pencil to make a note of the address and the way there as well as he could on a torn-off scrap of the telephone book cover before the Finn rang off in his hurry. His bent back, with its sprinkling of white hairs, was sweating

7

profusely. His usual old headache was already throbbing at his temples, it felt as if the bare bulb on his bedside table was piercing his head – the shade had fallen under the bed, and stretching down for it would have been even more painful. Not unusually he had drunk a whole bottle of aquavit the night before, sitting in front of an increasingly blurred television screen. Now it was coming again. But the headache could just as easily have come without the alcohol.

It had got more frequent in the last few years: it came on suddenly, with a white heat, sometimes when he bent down for something, sometimes when he woke up in the mornings. And often disappeared just as suddenly as it had come, strangely enough.

So the situation was clear, or as clear as it could be. They had had a tiler there, but something had happened to him, and now they were all hanging around waiting to get the tiles up on the walls. Tiles that were probably standing in piles of soggy fibreboard with loose metal bands around them out in the garden in the autumn mud. So why were they in such a hurry? Was it really just because they wanted to move in as quickly as possible? It was probably because they wouldn't get the next instalment of the loan if the building inspector hadn't been out there and seen that something had been done since the last one.

Torsten Bergman mulled it over. He was just about ready for a nice little job that wouldn't take up too many days. The bills were piling up on top of the fridge. Even the TV licence and the car insurance weren't paid.

And he had plenty of tiles, if it so happened that they were short over there. Heaps of tiles were lying around, as souvenirs of his work, his collected works, you could say, all over the place. Floor tiles of various thicknesses in the garden, because they could stand the winter cold better, wall tiles in the cellar.

He didn't like going down there nowadays, and when this abominably early telephone call had drilled into his aching head and tried to persuade him to take a tiling job, perhaps for the last time, it was the thought of having to go down into the cellar that put him off most.

Since the foul lavatory in the cellar had frozen up last winter there was always a lot of water down there, and it was no fun sticking your hands into the icy water to pick out what you wanted. It was always a damned nuisance when you had to fetch something from there. Tiles, for example.

He had definitely decided not to set foot down there since the lavatory froze up. He preferred to keep the door closed. The only thing he could remember more precisely at that moment was a wooden box with ten special tiles in, shaped as soap dishes. Putting them in bathrooms these days wasn't allowed, because elderly people might hurt themselves on them if they slipped in the bath. There was so much attention paid nowadays to all the dreadful accidents that could befall people. It was a shame; they were so wonderfully different from everything else he had around. And now no one would ever want them. He sometimes dreamed about how it might look if he set them close together, at regular intervals, along a single wall. It would look like the saw-toothed back of some kind of particularly dangerous sea-monster or dragon. But pranks like that were probably not what was expected of him.

Fairly heavy, handsome, plain Finnish tiles from the record years of the sixties. He'd had a great heavy lorry-load of them driven to his home, some time at the very beginning of the sixties, but the trouble with them was that they were so heavy that over the years they'd sunk deep down into the water-logged earth floor of the cellar. He would have had to dig

9

them up with a spade if he'd ever needed them. But it didn't much matter now.

He actually had hoards of tiles in the cellar if he could only manage to get himself down there and face the stench of the lavatory and open the door. Even if he didn't always know exactly where he should look for what. The oldest, from the Ekeby works near Uppsala, from the thirties onwards. All discreetly purloined, some just one or two at a time on the back of his cycle, in his lunch box. And they were really beautiful tiles. He'd always been so fond of his tiles.

The oldest of them were now so fashionable that they were copied by the finest Italian tile factories in Florence, Lucca and Vicenza, and were imported at great cost. Why fine tiles should be imported at high prices from abroad, when the buildings of the famous old Swedish factories were just used for therapy workshops for delinquent youths and drying-out clinics for local alcoholics – well, that was something beyond him.

After rather complicated negotiations with the General Insurance Company about his stomach, he'd been on sickness benefit for the last few years, and cashed his money order once a month in the post office at Rackarbacken. It was there he used to take his meagre offerings to pay off his mortgage loan in the glorious forties. We were happier then, he used to say, much happier than ever before or since. Or was he perhaps even happier as a little boy?

Although he lived only about fifteen hundred yards from the factory that had provided bread for himself and his wife and the boys for so long, he hadn't set foot in the semi-derelict buildings over there for years. It made him fearful and miserable just going near it and seeing little birch saplings and thistles sprouting up between the railway tracks where tipping wagons, loaded to the top with heavy local Uppland clay, had once run. Because it reminded him in a vague and general way of a time when his life had still been full of people.

He heaved himself up on his elbow towards a dawn that had still not arrived. The sound of dripping from the old rotting apple trees outside in the garden set off a cold shudder that went down his spine from bone to bone, as slow and meticulous as the very devil – as if he was well and truly meant to feel it.

The world was all around him, and nothing in that world was really his. So began Torsten Bergman's Thursday.

The house

IT WAS PERHAPS a little less cold than he had expected, but the air was damp and raw. When he stuck his nose out of the porch door his headache immediately began to ease off. Sometimes it disappeared with surprising speed, almost as if it had found someone else to attach itself to. Would it find its way home again after its trip out?

The autumn leaves that were never raked up had begun to form an interwoven carpet in the garden, and there rose from it a bitter smell of fermentation, decay and death. The question now was whether he would manage to start his old Volvo that he'd been given a year or two ago by his nephew, who felt sorry for him. It was standing among the piles of leaves almost as if it were part of the general decay. He actually had to scrape away a whole heap of leaves to get its creaking door open.

A rank odour of old rotting upholstery, stale viscous car oil and mortar came wafting up from the interior of the car as if it were its own bad breath.

It had a towing bracket and trailer, but it was very doubtful whether he could ever have got the trailer's indicators and brake lights to work properly.

Torsten Bergman only used the car when he was going to transport tools and material. Otherwise he preferred to cycle, leaving himself freer in more ways than one.

The old cover that lay across the bonnet probably did more harm than good on mornings like this. But at least some things thrived in the dank world beneath this strange firmament: centipedes and cockroaches and all imaginable kinds of beetles and creepy-crawlies, the sort that are hard to put a name to and that only the damp and darkness bring out. Without ceremony he threw the cover on top of the compost heap, tried to wipe the worst of the dew off the windscreen with his coat sleeve, and sat himself down in the musty smell of the car's interior. The devil alone knew whether it would start. He had no recollection at all of when he'd last driven it.

To his utter astonishment the car started immediately: it was a decent and well-behaved old car after all. There was a strange white cloud of smoke from burnt-out piston rings coming from the exhaust, and it soon looked as if it was filling the whole garden within the corrugated iron fence; but the engine was running like clockwork, and that was the main thing.

Getting out of the gate with the trailer on wasn't always easy. It was narrow across the muddy tracks that formed the driveway into the back garden, and now in the autumn it was so damned slippery that it was more luck than judgement if he could get the trailer through without one of its wheels catching on the fence post. And when he drove off it could be heard by every bloody neighbour in the district. Then they said he drank so much that he couldn't handle his car any more even when he was sober. And getting out had actually become a bit trickier over the years. Not so much because he drank – something that he indubitably did from time to time – but because he'd begun to have such damned trouble seeing. The eyes behind the old metal-framed glasses curling round his big frostbitten ears were red-rimmed, and constantly watering and sore. Why they had to be like that he had no idea.

Perhaps it was because he never cleaned his glasses these days. Since his wife died he'd seldom had a handkerchief in his pocket. Old newspaper didn't really do the job properly.

This would be a good morning if the damned car came out on the right tracks from the beginning, so to speak. It stood there now in all its rusty glory on the street, waiting and taking up space and making the whole bend dangerous. With the trailer as well. Only after he'd got out with it did he start thinking. Shouldn't he at least have a few tools with him? There would probably be no point getting any tiles out of the waterlogged cellar. And if it did turn out to be necessary, getting them up on the trailer would be a hell of a job.

But it would be pointless at the moment – before he knew how much was needed and what it would be for. Better to have some money in advance to get a few things together and start work in a more systematic way.

But tools? There must be something in the car from last time. It was hard to remember how many weeks might have passed since then. Though he had a distinct recollection of the hammer going missing in the last few days of the job. At the end he'd used the flat side of a monkey-wrench instead, and it hadn't really been as good. The devil alone knew what he still had lying about down in the cellar. He had an unfortunate tendency to lose half his tools on every job he undertook. He really couldn't face the idea of splashing around in the stagnant water down there.

He delved deep in his increasingly uncertain memory. There was a rusty old carpenter's hammer in the boot of the car, he was sure. And that would be good enough to chip off badly set or old tiles with, anyway. Once he got going he'd be needing tile cement and grouting in any case, and they'd have to give him some money to start him off. Then with a bit of luck he might be able to fit in a lunch-time visit to the liquor store at Luthagen on the way to the builders' merchants out at Bolanden. Already he could see the day before him in a more positive light.

There was a risk that they might not believe he was coming, and might send for someone else instead. So he'd have to leave now, with as little delay as possible. He didn't even have a sandwich with him. But that could be sorted out one way or another. The only thing he could see out in the kitchen was a good, reliable marking cord for lining up the tiles, and he quickly rolled it up and stuffed it in his pocket. He put a pair of dry socks in his jacket pocket, and dammit – if there wasn't an orange there too, even if it had gone a bit dry on one side from lying too long on the bench in the kitchen.

It wasn't a long drive over to Luthagen, and it was a nice one. He knew the district well. His father had even had an allotment down there by the river. And he'd gone fishing there for perch in the river as a little boy, right above the old swimming pool that had gone long ago, torn down and replaced by something new. That he'd never looked at very closely.

He didn't like real traffic, and particularly not police cars and all the other bloody things you met on the roads nowadays. He took an extra turning just to avoid Svartbäck Street where there were often police cars that might come after him and his jalopy with insolent and brutal questions about brake lights and inspection stickers and all the other crap those jerks had thought up. It was still fairly dark when he got to the house, but there was no doubt that it was the right house he'd come to, because the number was large and clear on the gable facing the street.

*

It was bigger than he'd thought. A rather large rendered house that must once have contained four small flats, and now after the renovation would probably have only two. This old part of town on the east side of the river was clearly starting to get posher now. The house had a good position behind a solid old-fashioned fir hedge, and the new yellow cement rendering was glowing. All the windows had evidently been changed too, because they had delivery markings pasted on the glass, and the frames were shiny aluminium.

It wasn't particularly difficult getting in through the gate-posts. But inside the garden, where the lawn had been churned up into mud by all the vehicles that had come and turned there, things didn't look quite so smart.

The sturdy old apple trees had got some hefty gashes from carelessly driven lorries, and there wasn't much left of the flower-beds. Even the edging stones had been really pressed down into the ground in places, as neat and level with the mud as if they'd been drawing-pins.

It would be pretty slippery to drive on to the churned-up grass.

Two young boys on mopeds were riding round the trees in meandering circles and came out right in front of Torsten's car. Torsten nearly collided with the second one, who looked as if he wasn't really awake. It was unnerving. The boy's frightened eyes gleamed white in the faint light, as white as the eyes of a dead fish. Torsten spat a curse from the car window, and the boys disappeared as fast as they'd come into sight.

Torsten Bergman was a sensitive man; he was susceptible to portents and premonitions.

He heaved himself laboriously up out of the car, checked that he still had the trailer with him and went with resolute steps up to the house.

The entrance door was dazzlingly new, made of beautifully varnished oak panels that must have cost quite a bit. It opened with no trouble at all, and Torsten Bergman stood in a newly painted entrance hall with a pleasantly fresh smell of paint from the walls and ceiling. A fine staircase, also made of oak, disappeared upwards in the darkness towards the top floor.

There seemed to be the sound of voices coming from up there. Or perhaps it was just voices from outside. The house was a cross between something very modern – you might say something modern that hadn't quite come off – and an old, dark labyrinth.

Down here everything was quiet.

But he'd found it, anyway. He had a job. Someone would turn up soon and explain to him what had to be done. And there'd be money and a bit of proper work for a few days. And perhaps some nice people to chat with in the coffee breaks.

He was already in a much better frame of mind.

Opus incertum

Torsten Bergman went into what seemed to be intended as his workplace. The whole thing seemed rather stylish and ambitiously planned. A big kitchen with masses of work-surfaces and a freestanding unit in the middle, glass-fronted cupboards and electrical sockets. The room opened out to the left.

Dining room, living room to the right, plasterboard, neatly stacked and covered with fibreglass sheeting, a couple of pasting trestles in the middle of a floor that must be newly laid, since it was covered with paper. There were probably more rooms further on, but it wasn't very easy to see in the dim light. There was a Thermos flask on a chair and a half-empty cup of coffee. It looked as if it had been there a long time. The coffee was cold, anyway. No, not just cold; the cup actually smelled mouldy. Torsten Bergman carefully spat out the sip he'd taken.

It got darker further in. Harder to find your way around. Perhaps some of the windows had been boarded up. Torsten felt rather unsure of himself as he kept coming upon door handles that opened readily into equally pitch-black rooms. When he thought about it, there had in fact been boards up at some of the windows on the outside. It was probably because they'd been spraying the rendering of the outside walls with an elegant antique-style paint, and obviously quite recently.

But the big room with its echoing sound and smell of tile cement, not yet completely dry if his nose wasn't mistaken – that must be the bathroom, for God's sake?

Or perhaps it was a laundry room. Or something completely different? Could it be a washroom? It wasn't easy to tell the difference in the dark. There was a wooden door h re and that would quite likely lead into a sauna. But was that really a bath? It looked almost as big as a small swimming pool, and if he hadn't watched out at the last minute he would have taken a step backwards right into it. With unimaginable consequences. God knows how long he could have been lying there at the bottom of the bath, or whatever it was, with a broken leg.

He could have died of hunger and thirst. Not a soul knew that he was there. Pentti was the only one who'd perhaps wonder where he'd got to and why he'd never turned up at the job he'd found for him. The boys on the moped would hardly worry about who he was or where he'd got to.

If there really were people living on the upper floor, as Pentti had said, they'd possibly smell the corpse down here eventually. If nobody turned up here to work, of course. But it didn't feel as if they would.

Almost instinctively he began to run his hands along the tiled wall. It wasn't easy to feel in the dark what sort of tiles they were; in any case not a type he recognised. It didn't really seem very well done. It felt as if the joins were uneven and rather as if a few of the tiles were crooked. Torsten groped his way further along, increasingly suspicious about the kind of people that could have been working here before him. There were electric switches here and there, but obviously not connected. Nothing happened however much you flicked them up and down.

Things would be a lot easier, thought Torsten, if he had

access to a lamp on an extension-lead. At the moment there was no way he could find out who he was really working for and what had to be done. Nor where he could get hold of materials and tools. But if he only had a lamp on an extension-lead, he would at least be able to get a first overall impression of the situation.

With some difficulty Torsten managed to get back out to more hospitable rooms that had some light from the autumn day outside. It was raining cats and dogs now. Even here in the dining room and living room it was so murky that he stumbled over abandoned buckets, an apparently pointless bundle of rags tried to wind itself round his right foot, and a step-ladder nearly fell on him.

All at once he was back by the stairs, looking again at the handsome door. Someone must have found a bargain somewhere. A door like that nowadays costs a pretty penny. And why had they put in so much work to make the ground floor so grand and elegant and left everything as it was on the upper floor? Standing down there in the stairway Torsten could see the point where the stylish new gold paint of the stairway stopped and was replaced by an old grey paint, and where careless tradesmen, or perhaps tenants, had made deep cuts and dents in the plaster everywhere.

Even the fine banisters suddenly stopped. A strangely incomplete building – at least, that was the impression it gave.

Was anyone intending to finish it?

He thought he could hear indistinct subdued noises from the upper floor. It was hard to tell whether it was a television that was on, or whether it was real people talking to one another. At one moment Torsten thought he could hear a child's voice, then there was something that sounded like a snatch of music, and then all the sounds became indistinct again. Perhaps it was just something coming from the street?

Since he was already at the foot of the stairs, he couldn't help creeping up to the top and looking at the doors. They were dirty brown. One had nothing on it, but on the other was a name.

Though instead of a name-plate there was just a piece of cardboard, fixed with a somewhat lopsided drawing-pin.

Sophie K. was all that was written on the card. What sort of people could they be, Torsten wondered, who don't dare write out their surname? Were they perhaps afraid of the tax authorities? Or could they be immigrants, perhaps some kind of refugees, who didn't have residence permits? Perhaps it might even be some sort of terrorist hide-out up here on the unrenovated top floor. He tried in vain to remember whether Pentti had said anything in particular about the upper floor, but if he had, he couldn't recall it.

Was there any chance that these people would have such a thing as a lamp on an extension-lead? Did ordinary people have such things at home? It wasn't easy to know things like that. It struck him that he didn't know very many ordinary people. In some way he'd finished with ordinary people after his wife died.

Torsten rang the doorbell. It seemed to be working. All was silent within.

"Good morning," said Torsten aloud to the closed door. "I'm here to do some tiling in the flat below. But the lights aren't working. Do you happen to know whether there's a lamp on an extension-lead in the house?"

No answer. Could it possibly be a child he was talking to? The silence began to be painfully long.

Torsten began to think about all the least pleasant possibilities of the situation. Perhaps he might be running the risk of being misunderstood as some kind of dirty old man, trying to get to know little girls while their parents were out? Perhaps a mad assailant would come rushing out with a weapon at any moment?

The door remained as silent as before. Whoever Sophie K. might be, she wasn't a particularly communicative person.

As he stepped slowly and thoughtfully back down the stairs he was listening, almost against his will, in case the door might yet be opened inquisitively and closed again. But no such sound was to be heard.

In a mixture of desperation and absent-mindedness Torsten went out to the garden. It was as muddy and churned up as before, but the rain had eased off a little. The car and trailer were still standing where he'd left them. There was just as little trace of the owner or contractor out there as inside the house. A slow goods train on its way to Gävle, or perhaps to the silent and harmless north, clattered past on the other side of the road. He felt rather as if he'd quite like to be on it. There was a pungent scent in the air, of rotting leaves, of the sluggish yellow river flowing by not far away, a scent that almost seemed to him to be the raw scent of time itself, moving through the world. Or was it the world moving through time?

Occupied with these thoughts, but also with peeing against a leafless ornamental bush by the wall, Torsten Bergman noticed the electricity fuse box, fastened to the house wall at a man's height, right in front of his nose. Its door was half open. With a bit of luck it might just be that someone had simply turned off the main switch! But how was Sophie K. managing in the top flat in that case? Was she really sitting in the dark up there? And who was she anyway? Perhaps a pretty young mother of several children. He imagined her with red hair, a high bosom and three little children clinging to her skirt. Perhaps he would eventually manage to meet her?

He inspected the contents of the fuse box dreamily and short-sightedly. So that was why there hadn't been any damned lights in the house! Every single one of the four main fuses was missing! And then there were several cables and other oddities that Torsten didn't understand. Of course he'd handled boxes like this before on building jobs, but he wasn't particularly clued up on unapproved connections and the like. But what the hell – it wouldn't be so very difficult to buy a fuse or two and put them in. He had a bit of money in his inside pocket. He moved off resolutely towards the Volvo. The engine was still warm and it started first time. He took the trailer with him to be on the safe side.

It was raining more heavily again now. He had to go right down to Svartbäcken and double-park in a dangerous position in a side street, jeered and sworn at by the crew of a garbage truck that he must have held up for a quarter of an hour while he was in the electrical shop hunting around for the damned fuses. He tried to give as good as he got, but he wasn't really in a frame of mind to be abusive that day. Everything seemed so odd to him. But now he had the fuses safely in his inside pocket.

And it was already half past ten, almost lunch time. Damned funny what a peculiar quality time had of either going too fast or too slow.

As he put in the fuses, one after another, his coat and cap soaked through with the rain, he thought to himself that either the damned thing would have to work now or the whole bloody business could go to hell.

But it worked! The lights came on! The first thing he noticed was a light in the windows of the top floor, up there where that strange lady Sophie K. must live. And on the ground floor everything suddenly fell into place: there were at least a few bulbs here and there. The rooms and their relationship to each other began to come clear to Torsten Bergman. And of course everything seemed a bit smaller now; he realised how he'd gone in circles and come out in the same room all the time. There wasn't much lighting, just the occasional bare bulb – but enough for him to manage.

It was quite a large bathroom, and divided into various sub-sections, so to speak. It really was rather grandly conceived. And stylish. With the bath-tub itself in the middle and sunk into the floor. Very fine. With a really neat sauna and a little changing room to the left. And to the right was what was to be the laundry room, and that was to have tiled walls too, as it should have. The floor felt well-laid anyway, they were decent floor tiles from the Pertillä factory in Finland.

Torsten ran his hand along the walls, and what he could now see came as rather a surprise. It looked as if several different people had been doing this bathroom, some good, some dreadful botchers, working around each other, and none taking any account of the others' work. The only thing they had in common was that they all seemed to have had plenty of material.

It started off all right by the door. Well-cemented and neat joins and the little pieces along the door-frame really splendidly fitted in. Excellent Finnish tiles, quite substantial in fact. And they'd even gone to the expense of a fine blue border.

But the weird thing about this back wall that Torsten was now following in the light of the rather paint-spattered bulb, was the way it became more and more unrecognisable and unlike its true self the further from the door he got. First the joins became increasingly uneven. It was as if the man setting the tiles had suddenly lost his plumb line, or had panicked at the thought that his grouting was about to run out. Then a section began where black grouting had been used instead of the light type, which was obviously the only right one to use. It made a curiously pathetic impression, because the change didn't come all at once, but gradually, as if the light grouting had been mixed with more and more of the dark as the light one had begun to run out. How had these people thought they could get away with such a slovenly job!

And further on, along the half-finished short wall, it suddenly got even worse. Tiles broken in the middle where two or sometimes even three parts had been badly joined together to make one. And where some missing pieces had simply been replaced by tile cement. It looked really horrific. Not even a council housing department would have found work like that acceptable.

Torsten gave a little shudder. It almost frightened him to see work that had been started with all the best intentions and then, for God knows what reason, allowed to end up in the most grotesquely uneven and scruffy mess.

He felt uneasy. The peculiar thing was not just that his predecessor had so clearly lost heart (of course, one not entirely implausible theory was that he had slowly but surely got himself drunk in the course of the work) but that he (or they?) didn't seem to have any idea of *how* much the work had changed and deteriorated along the way. And it struck him that things were quite often like that with many lives. Or was it perhaps really that all lives looked like that if you held a light up to them and examined them closely enough? Was there any life of which you could say that it improved as time went on? Didn't the bad habits get worse, the compromises more fudged, the inconsistencies greater? In short, wasn't this life always a slow journey from a little order to an ever greater disorder?

If indeed it had been one and the same person working here. But if there had been more of them, wouldn't they probably have got into a fight? Or perhaps you could imagine that they'd taken over from one another as contractors changed or fell out with their tilers?

Torsten tried to shake off these thoughts as quickly as he could. Something had to be done here. And really there was no question about how it had to be done. It simply meant taking down the whole damned lot and starting all over again from the point where everything had gone wrong. (Whether it was possible to decide *where* it had begun to go wrong was another matter, of course.) There was any number of tiles in neat bundles with metal bands over in the corner. There should – as far as his eye could estimate – be just about enough. In any case, there'd be enough to work with today and tomorrow. And there'd be time to get tile cement and grouting, if he could only get hold of the contractor.

The fact that the contractor hadn't yet turned up to explain how he wanted things done was an obvious stumbling block. And he hadn't sent anyone else, either, a foreman or some-one. All there was for it was to guess what was intended and do his best.

You hardly ever knew for sure what was expected of you.

Still, Torsten knew from experience that people like that are never in much of a hurry. It had once taken a whole week before he'd met the man he was working for. That time it had been an office on Vaksala Street, and the job was simpler.

Was it possible that the contractor, or someone who knew how he wanted it done, had looked in while he was out buying the fuses?

On the other hand, things were fairly clear-cut here. First a few square yards of completely useless, disastrous handiwork had to be hacked off with a hammer. And then of course the tile cement that was still sticking to the wall would have to be chiselled off.

It was always worse, Torsten thought, to take over from someone else than to start from scratch. But that's just what you damned well have to do all the time when you work like this, in the background, *an outcast in the twilight world of illicit work*, he thought, pleased with the dramatic sound of his own phrase.

Taking over where others had cleared out and left things half done and botched. Taking over what they hadn't finished off before they went on to the next job – or like the one before me here, whoever the devil he was, before they got too drunk or too bleary-eyed to finish the whole thing off, and thrown out by the beginning of the afternoon.

The hammer was lying in the metal box where it should be. Finding a proper chisel wasn't so easy, but there was a reliable old screwdriver there that would do.

All that remained was to set to work. The bad tiling came splintering off and shards flew past Torsten's face, but he was used to that. Lucky that he had his old glasses in the breast pocket of his leather jacket. There was a healthy – or rather, unhealthy – cloud of dust all round him, but he was used to that, too. It was beautiful to see all this hideousness disappearing bit by bit and being replaced by the plain rough wall surface with no more of the awful shoddy work left on it. Only the great weals of his screwdriver.

But it was just good to see something being done.

Hypotheses about Sophie K.

WHEN I'VE HACKED OFF about another square yard, Torsten said to himself with surprising decisiveness, I'll go up and see that Sophie K., whoever she is, and try to tell her I'm not dangerous. On the contrary, I'm a warm and friendly man that she'd enjoy getting to know.

We'd both enjoy sitting down at her kitchen table, and she'd make me a cup of coffee and some sandwiches. (One cheese and one liver paste and cucumber.)

Sophie would be in her thirties, a pretty woman, but perhaps slightly on the plump side, dressed in a blue house-coat. You wouldn't have any idea what she might have on under the house-coat.

Sophie would be a young painter; there'd be a glimpse of her easel and her whatsitsname with all the paints on through the kitchen door. There'd be several of her paintings (very hard to fathom but in strong, bright colours) decorating the walls in there, and her carelessly-made bed.

Sophie would explain that she was only living there temporarily (since she'd just come through a very harrowing divorce) and she'd borrowed this flat while they were waiting for the refurbishment work to come on up to the top floor. She knew the owner slightly. Yes, there was nothing wrong with the owner. It was he who was both owner and builder. He went in for this kind of business a little: doing places up and selling them again and making lots of money in the process. (That's to say, lots of money if he somehow managed to avoid the tax, of course.) But he was good at that. He was in the habit of driving up here on Friday afternoons in a BMW to see whether everything was all right. Yes, she couldn't deny that he did take her out for a drink, now and then. But Torsten shouldn't draw any hasty conclusions from that, she added quickly, and crossed her legs decisively so that Torsten couldn't peer up her skirt. (Was the sandwich OK? Would he like another?)

No, there was nothing wrong with the owner. But the annoying thing was that he had a hard job getting good people to work for him. Last time there'd been a non-stop coming and going. One tiler had taken over where another had stopped, and each was worse than the last. Men who obviously had no idea what they were doing and who took the money they'd got for material to buy themselves drink. Got themselves drunk, they did, before they'd done half a day's work.

It was really nice to see that a sensible person had finally arrived who could do a proper job. She said that because she was thinking of the owner, poor old Hasse from Tierp. For herself it was a good thing that it was going slowly. She really didn't know where she'd be able to go once the work started coming up to the top floor.

Then Torsten would start talking about his own house at Kungsgärdesplan (the size and other merits of which he would exaggerate slightly). Yes, it was a good house. But that too was in need of repair. Just that for a hard-working craftsman there was seldom any spare time for getting on with his own things. They had to come last. So obviously there was quite a lot that needed doing. And would soon be done, too. It was just that there had been so much happening lately. Yes. So many things. Trouble of one sort or another.

When you're a widower you don't have so much spare time. Or perhaps you do.

Sophie K., a surprisingly beautiful red-haired woman in a black velvet dress, opened the door to Torsten Bergman.

She scrutinised him carefully. Torsten was conscious of the dreadful amount of tile dust he must have on his overalls. He glanced down at his baggy knees and they looked absolutely terrible. Sophie K. was very pale. She had big, blue, slightly frightened eyes, and a look of determination around her mouth.

"What do you want? You must be new. Why have they sent you now? You're not the usual one."

"What do you mean by *the usual one?*"

"Well, the usual one, the one those damned builders send here to make a noise and upset me and drive me out of here."

"What *damned builders?*"

"Those bloody builders from Stockholm."

"I don't know them."

"But you must do. Since you're working for them. You don't fool me. They've sent you here, admit it."

"To tell the truth, I've got no idea who I'm working for. A mate rang and said there'd been some trouble with a job and that I should jump in. What's so special about this house, then?"

"You don't mean you don't know what's going on? They're drug dealers, all of them. And then they launder their money with property like this. They do it up a bit and then sell it on half-finished."

"No, I had no idea."

(Was the suspicion in her eyes a sign that she was mad? Perhaps he had a madwoman to deal with. Mad or not, she was devilishly attractive in her way. Wasn't there something very attractive about madwomen? And wasn't it the fact that they were really *capable of anything*? This woman was capable of doing anything. Throwing a bottle in his face or dragging him in and throwing him down on the carelessly made-up couch, and digging her sharp nails into his back. God knows what she might force him to do.)

Sophie K. scrutinised him even more carefully, or so it seemed.

"I'm beginning to believe you," she said, very slowly and deliberately. "You obviously don't know what types you're dealing with. And I can see that for one very simple reason. You have no idea what they'd do with you if they discovered that you were keeping company with me. Imagine if they found us in bed here, if the owner caught us fucking in the bed in broad daylight – something I rather think you'd like to do – wouldn't you?"

"I'm not really sure," Torsten thought he should answer, stuttering a little.

"Quite honestly I don't think that either of us would come out alive," said Sophie K. *Either of us.* They're dangerous, you can be sure of that. Very dangerous. And they might turn up at any time. You can also be sure of that. Any time at all. Just drive up here in the garden in their big BMW. You seldom hear the owner and his friends come. They're very quiet on the stairs. It's a kind of habit of theirs."

"I don't give a shit about them," said Torsten, and strode decisively into the room. "I'm man enough to take care of you, little girl, and of them."

*

31

This notion made him hammer at his tiled wall with even heavier blows and a pounding heart.

The person who came to open the door this time sounded as if she was moving with very slow, even shuffling, steps. Torsten wasn't at all surprised when a white-haired old woman, so old that she looked shrivelled up by the years, slowly opened the door. Obviously her sight wasn't very good either.

"What do you want?" she asked, as if she too was not in the least surprised at his knock.

"Are you Sophie K.?" Torsten asked.

"Yes, you can see I am."

"Why don't you put up your surname?"

"Well, you know, that's rather a long story. If I were to tell you, you probably wouldn't get much more done today. Would you like to come in, by the way? I've just put the coffee on, as it happens. I always have a little coffee about this time of day, you see."

A pleasant smell of coffee brewing, of an old lady's little flat with pelargoniums in the windows and a peacefully sleeping cat in the corner of the sofa. An embroidered sampler on the kitchen wall. This woman didn't seem in the least surprised at anything.

"You want to borrow a lamp with an extension-lead? But I don't have things like that, you know. My husband had a lot of things, but when he went off I gave most of it away. Gave it away. I could have sold it all, of course, but in fact I gave the whole lot away. For nothing."

She looked him over with her old yet observant eyes.

"So you're Torsten Bergman."

"How can you know that?"

"It's easy enough. I knew you as a little boy in Hallsta.

When you lived with your uncle, the one with the metalwork business. I remember you very well. To think that you don't seem to remember me!"

And at that point Torsten would look at the old lady's face very carefully: the deep wrinkles under her eyes, her nose covered with liver spots, her thin dry lips.

Slowly the light would dawn on him.

"But aren't you Aunt Sophie? Aunt Sophie Karlsson from the telephone exchange?"

"Of course I am. Nice that you remembered me. Don't you remember taking a photograph of Lisa and me once at the telephone exchange? You were very good with a camera then. Do you remember how interested you were in photography?"

Of course Torsten remembered. Better than usual, it seemed to him. The metalworker's house under the big elm trees, the back garden where the dogs used to play, Buster and Pan, and him rushing around on the grass with them on free afternoons while his mother was cleaning at the bank. The strange noises from inside the workshop where his strict uncle had forbidden him to set foot. And doing the long-jump in the gravel in front of the workshop on summer evenings with the apprentices (it was the summer of the Olympics) for hours on end it seemed, without any of them admitting to tiredness or defeat. They used to run and wrestle too.

Otherwise Torsten at the age of sixteen was in general a serious little fellow. He went to English classes on Wednesdays and set up his own darkroom in a cubby-hole up in the metalworker's attic. While times were good and the workers bought enough in Strand's shop at the front of the metal-worker's house, he could afford to carry on with his developing and making paper prints from the plates. He took in a few orders for photographs, too. From his mother's friends at the chapel.

Aunt Sophie knew about all that. Just to think that she was still alive! With flowers in her windows exactly as before, and the smell of coffee, and the cat. He would hold out his hand carefully as he sat there with his cup of coffee and his cheese sandwich and offer it the last tiny bit of the sandwich. It would feel exactly as it did when he was a little boy. What an extraordinarily long way he'd come from that world, where he was still a serious little chap who delivered newspapers in the mornings and worked in Strand's shop in the afternoons and wanted to be a photographer just like Nilson down in Sörstafors.

But now his damned stomach was hurting again. He recognised that too from his youth. Though it had got worse over the years – that he had to admit.

Torsten Bergman had never really had a very good relationship with his stomach.

He could still remember how much it could hurt between the ages of twelve and fifteen, when he had to go to school. And it got even worse when he was sixteen, on cold winter mornings when he had to go out in the snowdrifts, shovel snow from in front of the shop (where he worked in the afternoons), dig out his bike from its rack and then go off to the station to collect the morning papers that had to be delivered.

It wasn't always much fun. Least of all on winter mornings when he had to get down to the station at five o'clock to collect the bundle of papers. He, Torsten, used to take the papers out on a big old bike of his mother's. The paperboys used to stand in a freezing, shivering group out on the platform waiting for the morning train from Västerås to come in.

There was no warm waiting room for them: it wasn't open at that time of the morning.

Sometimes he had the feeling of having stood waiting all his life to be let into a warmer room. And no door had ever really wanted to open for him.

There were interesting things and there were boring things.

There was the shop with the stern Misses Molander who owned it. Every morning the snow had to be shovelled away outside so that, as they used to say, people wouldn't break their legs. After real February storms there could be quite a lot of shovelling to be done. The winter of 1933, when he was sixteen, was the worst. Shovelling snow from six in the morning and chopping wood in the evening in the metal-worker's yard until it was time to collapse into bed.

The shop was either half-full of people – that was when it was pay day at the factory, and all the wives came streaming in to fill up their bags in the grocer's with American meat and fat herring and bags of flour – or it was strangely half-empty for days on end. Then the Molander sisters would withdraw sullenly into the little inner room, the *Office* as they called it, and quarrel quietly together.

Of course there were interruptions and sudden inspections and ideas that something or other should be cleaned or counted (Why hadn't Torsten dusted the counters?), but there was always enough time to devote to interesting things. Listening to the wireless, and cameras. That is, you could read about the wireless in "Science and Life" magazine that you could borrow from the library. If you were going to listen to the wireless, it had to be on the smart little receiver at Reverend Fors' house. A fantastic feeling to hear music and voices from across the seas! Ghostly, as if there was a spirit world somewhere out there. But easy to explain when you sat down and read about it. About radio waves and frequency modulation and the strange ability of short waves to bounce off the very highest levels of the atmosphere and come back down to earth in the most unexpected places. And the interesting thing about a needle against a crystal letting an electric current pass in only one direction. (If that was how "Science and Life" explained it.) On days when conditions were right you could hear German and English spoken on the wireless set. And you could hear Kalundborg in Denmark quite often.

The wireless was a sort of counter-balance to the spiritual stuff that Mother went in for, the Evangelical Society and revivalist meetings and auctioning parcels for the chapel. Torsten kept up contact with another world, too, but in a more modern, more scientific way, so to speak. (But when you heard Bratislava through the ionospheric fading of a winter evening for ten minutes or so, you might well ask who was involved in the more supernatural activity.) At least there was always a gentle fragrance of coffee floating around Mother's supernatural pursuits and her incomprehensible Jesus. His own higher life floated entirely on its own in the invisible winter air.

Looking through a camera had the opposite effect. It enlarged the visible area. Mother was equally against both. She detested both cameras and crystal wireless sets. Because they meant throwing away hard-earned money on useless things. (Oh, he was a confirmed teetotaller at that time, though mostly through lack of experience of what it was all about. If she had been able to see him today she would have had other things to complain of. But Mother died in the forties.) Fundamentally, though, it wasn't a question of the money but the fact that she'd got a kind of unexpected competition in spiritual matters.

His first camera was a pin-hole camera that he'd made himself, the second was a Zeiss box camera. There was nothing or everything to photograph: the bare and empty street in winter with its snowdrifts, the leafless maple trees on Knektbacken Hill (where you could still see the wind-torn remnants of his kite), the stylish new Post and Telegraph Office. The really interesting and important part was not what pictures you took. The main thing was the developing.

In the glow of the red lamp up in the attic, in the gentle spray from the suspended watering can, just as the very first shadows began to emerge in the developing liquid, that was when he would feel something that must have been happiness. The transition from pale, vague shadows to pictures obviously took place as gradually and imperceptibly as plants growing. It was astonishing that the world could work like that. In a way he couldn't easily describe in words, it reminded him of himself.

Where could those yellowing old photographs on cheap paper be now? Perhaps they were simply at the bottom of a drawer somewhere up in his own attic? There was so much there that had been put away over the course of the years, never to be opened again.

The whole concept of the blackness that gradually emerges in the developing tank was inextricably linked with those days, the years of his boyhood, when he was slowly beginning to recover from a cold. The first unaccustomed feeling of no longer being feverish, the faint rough contours of the world taking shape again on days like that.

Torsten had had a dreadful number of illnesses as a little boy. He actually began by getting Spanish 'flu at the age of two. For some unknown reason he didn't die of it, and so things went on in the same way almost up to puberty, when his body – as surprisingly for himself as for his schoolfellows, who still carried on believing he was easy prey for their beating – began to get firm, tough and wiry. But all those days when he used to lie in bed with a fever looking up at the brown wallpaper, as the hours dragged past with the shadows outside the window, all those pains in tonsils and lungs, all those strange rashes and spots: what was the point of them? The little schooling he'd got had been interrupted by all his days of sickness, they had been bad for his self-confidence because he was usually so tired and weak in the playground that even children from classes below him had been able to beat him up. But they had also given him a secret life, one that was his own.

How would he have been able to go on without his other, his secret life?

Lunch break

THE SOUND OF a new heavier shower of rain closed the doors of his imagination and brought him back to emptiness. He suddenly stopped working, right in the middle of a hammer-blow.

On top of everything else, his stomach had begun to hurt him again.

The broken pieces of tile were now so deep that they crunched under his feet as he walked out to the stairway, still bent double with the sudden stomach pain, and listened for sounds from the floor above. But all was silence. Perhaps it had just been the wind buffeting the door? Or perhaps the protective paper on one of the windows had come loose in the strong gusts.

And as for the card on the door, mightn't that be an old one? Who knew when Sophie K. had made off? Maybe even years ago?

He stepped over to the outside door and opened it. It was absolutely silent out there. Just the wind in the trees and a car going along the street.

Should he go upstairs again to look for Sophie K.? He felt he knew her a little better now.

But the pain in his stomach could be borne no longer. Perhaps it would be best if he had something to eat anyway. Really and truly there wouldn't be much to do in an hour or two. What had to be chipped off the wall would be done by then. And if no representative of the contractor or owner had come he'd be standing around with nothing to do unless he could get hold of some tile cement and grouting somehow or other. And a trowel. And a plumb line? Did he have one with him, or had he dreamed it?

He really and truly had no idea who it could be up there now. What sort of people could it be who'd just sit on their backsides and not answer when they're spoken to? Perhaps people who were up there illicitly and had nothing whatever to do with the house? Some boys who were just waiting for him to leave so that they could go on stealing things from the ground floor? Really and truly everything was completely unguarded down here. Or perhaps even worse – drug addicts or criminals? It suddenly felt uncomfortable being there. He'd worked so energetically for the last hour that he'd kept himself warm – but now he could feel that there actually wasn't any real warmth in the house.

Without any prior warning Torsten suddenly felt rather giddy. He went back to the bathroom on shaky legs and rinsed his face over the washbasin. That felt a bit better. He noticed for the first time that the taps were actually very expensive ones, unusually high-quality German Poggenpohl taps. That sort cost at least two or three hundred crowns each. Maybe more.

Including the one in the bidet, there was at least twelve hundred crowns sitting here doing nothing; that is, nothing for the moment. If Torsten was to get the work done, he had to have money for materials. What would be more natural than to unscrew a couple of taps, take them over to the builders' merchants out in Bolanden and exchange them for cash? That way no valuable working time would be lost and it would be the simplest thing in the world for the contractor to buy them back and screw them on again.

Torsten was no stranger to plumbing work, and his pipe-wrench was out in the Volvo, he was sure of that.

The nuts were new, so they came off as easily as anything. For the first one of course he made the mistake of not turning off the flow underneath first, so there was a lot of water before he got the situation under control. Two taps would be enough to get a sufficient advance for the materials he needed. Then the contractor could get them back again. If he couldn't turn up and look after his workers he ought to be grateful to have found a man of initiative who could look after himself.

Torsten drove out to the industrial area at Bolanden with a slight pain around his heart. It was the sort of pain he often felt after the strain of making a decision.

Linked by muddy lanes, the factories were in enclosures surrounded by high fences of varying heights, most of them topped with barbed wire. And behind the fences you could catch glimpses of piled-up objects: rusty machinery, gleaming new tractors, stacks of scrap metal. Heavy tractor-trailer trucks splashed through the mud. That was the sort of life people lived, and they knew nothing of any other lives.

The buildings weren't real buildings. They were constructions, flat plates of various kinds hung over metal frames joined together. These modern warehouses and workshops were almost entirely without windows, and it was striking that there were so few people to be seen. Just vehicles, warehouses and machinery. Somewhere on one of the sites a fork-lift truck was moving in the rain, and an old man could be seen rooting about in a box of odds and ends of pipe as if he were searching for something really special. Otherwise the whole area might have been uninhabited. Only at the vehicle-testing centre was there a long queue of not particularly new or fashionable cars waiting their turn. It looked like a kind of retirement home for old models that had once, at the beginning of the sixties, been gleaming and shiny.

I wonder, Torsten said to himself, whether new cars ever come to the test centre nowadays. Torsten shivered in his own chilly Volvo; he no longer knew how many months behind he was with his own car test. He probably wasn't allowed to drive it any longer after this amount of time. He'd stuffed the brown reminder away on top of the fridge where he used to put everything he intended to open later.

The industrial area went on for mile after mile. All the buildings were the same height, except for the power station that towered massively over everything else, and all the streets were interchangeable. When Torsten was young there had been nothing here but fields. That was in the days when he used to cycle out with his wife to drink coffee and look at the birds by the upper reaches of the river Före. We really took our pleasures in quite different ways in those days from the way people do now, he said to himself. Or do people have any pleasures at all nowadays? It struck him that he didn't have much knowledge of what other people got up to these days. And the worst thing was that he didn't much care either.

So this is trade and industry, Torsten said to himself. Properly divided into the correct parcels of land and constructed according to building regulations and never built more than two storeys high, just as it should be. And of course with toilets for the handicapped and properly arranged washrooms where the poor workers could slip off for a smoke when things got too tedious. It was very nice not to have things organised like that for yourself. People who work here have everything organised for them – taxes and insurance contributions and pensions and things. That's different, that is, from the underground economy where yours truly works. There you don't even know any more who you're working for or how you'll get the materials for the next few hours' work. There's a helluva difference between them and us who work *illegally*. Us criminal workers. Doesn't illegal mean criminal? To think that ordinary simple work should eventually end up as a crime! You couldn't have imagined that at the time you were learning that it was honourable to work. He cast a swift glance at the taps. Yes, they were still there, chrome-plated and stylish on the seat beside him. He'd probably manage to get the money for them all right.

The builders' merchant's was full of people as usual. Torsten said hello to a few carpenters that he'd known for years. Some greeted him back and asked where he was living now. Others seemed to be in such a hurry that they didn't have time to notice him. The assistant had a bit of trouble because Torsten couldn't give the account number; but with a little insistence it was done. This was a place that had lots of craftsmen as customers, and they were used to improvising. But the taps were in first-class condition, so there couldn't really be a problem. Tile cement and grouting and a few tools were fixed up in a matter of moments, and there was even money over that Torsten carefully stuffed into his back pocket. In an envelope with proper notes of debit and credit. It looked as if the damned rain would soon stop now.

He ought to thank God that at least there were tiles at the job. The price tiles had gone up to over the last few years, he'd have never got anywhere otherwise. You had to be able to improvise if you were going to get anything done in this business, he said to himself.

*

On the stroke of twelve Torsten walked into the Esso transport café out by the roundabout leading to the Stockholm road. There was a long queue, but it was moving quickly. The Finnish girls at the counter were speedily and efficiently dishing up beef and cabbage and pork sausage and everything else they had to the line of hungry long-distance lorry drivers and others. It was a perfectly-functioning establishment of its type, Torsten thought, taking ages to make up his mind between the beef and cabbage and pork sausage.

He decided in the end on the sausage, and it was impossible to resist taking one of the succulent Danish pastries with the wonderful yellow custard in that were set out at the end of the counter. For one brief moment Torsten felt like a happy consumer.

Now, surrounded by people again, he felt very much better. Coming out of that lonely building was almost like coming out of a prison, he said to himself.

The girls at the counter must have thought he was a bit slow and fussy when choosing his food. But they were friendly anyway, even though they were sweating and rushed off their feet, and they had small slim breasts under their aprons. He was still so covered in dust that most of the people in the queue kept a careful distance from him. He probably ought to have thought of the dust before he came in. Most of the customers were wearing smart overalls with various firms' names on the back. And there were a few with suits and briefcases. "Can you tell me how to get to Örbyhus?" one of them asked. Torsten started on a very detailed description, mentioned several interesting side roads where he used to go fishing for crayfish in the fifties, and was just beginning a description of the beautiful factory at Löfsta with its remarkable organ when he was interrupted, rather abruptly:

"You're crazy," the man said, his eyebrows slightly raised. "I've got five shops to visit in one afternoon. *I've got to step on the gas.*"

Torsten was so impressed by this expression '*step on the gas*' that he took his leave of the man with the greatest respect. Although he perhaps didn't really understand what it meant, it was an expression that he would seriously consider adopting for the future: '*I've got to step on the gas!*' It sounded so unsentimental and effective and urgent.

The pains in his stomach gradually wore off as the splendid meal went down. Perhaps it was simply food that I needed, he said to himself. I probably ought to think about my food a bit more. And when they began to come back again with the Danish pastry and the coffee, it was in a very much milder form anyway. Just as a vague memory and reminder of what they'd been before. His eyes, which were slightly red and irritated from all the tile dust, were attentively examining the pattern of the purple oilcloth on the table, examining the pattern because they didn't have anything else in particular to look at. The low, heavy cloud over the extensive industrial area of Bolanden looked as if it was slowly thinning. Perhaps there'd be a little sunshine in the afternoon after all?

"Well – isn't that Torsten? And where the devil have you been, then, with all that dust on you?"

Torsten looked up. A tall, thin figure in jeans and a tee-shirt with the words SANDVIKEN SAWS on it was leaning over the table. His hands were red and rough as if they'd been out too long in icy weather. His hair was thin and white across his high narrow forehead, and he had a pair of glasses on his nose with unusually thick lenses.

Torsten's face lit up.

"Well, if it isn't Stiggsy! What the hell are you doing here? Shouldn't you be in Morgongåva?"

"Weren't any jobs in Morgongåva. Hopeless. A lot's happened since I lived there. Wait a minute, I'll just get a coffee."

And Torsten watched Stig moving swiftly between the tables with his strange forward-leaning gait, heading towards a cup of coffee he must have left behind somewhere on the way. Torsten had known Stig Clason, his cousin, since they were boys. They'd jumped the long-jump together and delivered newspapers in crunchy new snow on icy mornings in the forties in Hallstahammar. A time when it was easy to sell newspapers.

Then Stig had come and gone. You might say. He was really a carpenter, if you can tell what a person *really* is. But that was only one of his many parts. He was, it suddenly occurred to Torsten, *a man of many parts*. There are also men of great depths, but that was a different matter. Stig had no great depths, but he had many parts. In the fifties he'd gone in for motorcycle racing. The sort of motorbikes you ride on the ice, with sharp spikes on the tyres, and where you put your knee down on the ice. Torsten couldn't for the life of him remember what it was called. But anyway he hadn't made it to the Swedish championships.

It was also said that he'd been a preacher for a while, something that didn't surprise Torsten. Stiggsy was a man of many parts. And he'd always had philosophical interests. And he used to be a good singer as well in those days. But as various older relations had died off, the reports about Stig had become few and far between. Once he'd been in Gothenburg working in the shipyards and earning pots of money. Then he'd finished with the shipyards in Gothenburg and he was with some firm up in Uddevalla that was building oil platforms. Then the oil rush was over, and the latest was that he was a carpenter in Morgongåva. He'd never seemed to manage to hang on to his wife and children. Torsten knew from various rumours that he'd been married at least twice. But since Aunt Selma over in Sala had died, the reports had been a bit patchy.

Just as a huge lorry and trailer darkened the view from the window – and it was one of those damned TIRs from Poland that rumour had it the bloody Russians used for spying on Swedish defence systems – we were living in funny times – Stig came back. He looked as if he'd got more short-sighted over the years.

"How are things with you, then?"

"Not too good. I'm on sickness benefit. It's my stomach that keeps playing up."

"And you've stayed in Uppsala all these years?"

"Yes, that's the way things went. Even after the wife died."

"And what's all this dust you've got on your trousers, then?"

"Chiselling. There's a house down by the teacher-training college divided into four flats that's being converted into two. Posh as hell. What's already done. But some idiots before me had messed it up. So I'm re-doing the bathroom and kitchen. The last tiler had mucked it up good and proper. There's some funny types about nowadays. It looked damned awful. Funny times nowadays. Good to have something to do. But the place is pretty lonely. Somehow. I started this morning and haven't seen a single soul out there yet. The sods haven't bothered to say what they want done. And I haven't had any money for materials, either. But you have to get by as best you can. What are you doing, then? Are you working for Sandviken Saws?"

"No, that's just the shirt. I'm getting on all right. It's just that I had a free day today. I had to take the car to be tested and it failed. The brakes were a bit old. So I had to take it in for repair. You have to take the rough with the smooth."

"Yes, you do. Well, I can drive you into town. I've got a lot to do today. *I've got to step on the gas*, you know!"

There was really so much Torsten wanted to ask about. He hadn't seen this fellow since they used to jump in the lock basin at Berg on summer evenings and swim, to the anger of the bargemen. They must have been sixteen when Mother fell out with the Clasons and moved to her sister's in Uppsala. And a kind of paradise had been lost. Yes, a sort of paradise of small dusty country roads with wild strawberries growing on the banks of the roadside ditches, hot summer days when the thunderstorms moved off over the forests to the north and it was great to throw themselves into the icy waters of the lock basins. Between high echoing stone-block walls. And water so black that a boat-hook was invisible a few inches down.

The blow of moving to Uppsala with its clayey fields and boring flat land without any lakes, only interrupted by the gloomy Crown Ridge and river Fyris, that ridiculous little stream, with freezing winters and snowstorms blowing through strangely empty streets, he'd really felt it. But, as with all loss, the years passed by and he'd stopped thinking about it.

Life was the way it was, and turned out the way it turned out. And you couldn't go back and repair it, either. Life was wretched.

No longer so alone

IT HAD REALLY BEEN rather horrible over there.
Now it wasn't so lonely any more.

Here he sat in the Volvo with another thin, white-haired, old man who had actually been there from the beginning. He had someone to talk to. It was a surprise, and he didn't know whether it made him happy or sad. The fact was that this man Stig must have seen him in a more pristine condition. Once upon a time.

It wasn't easy to talk about what they had in common. But it had to be done.

He'd also seen Stiggsy in a more pristine condition, of course. Stiggsy was laughing quietly to himself as he wiped the mist off the windscreen with the back of his hand. It was always the same damned trouble with this car: it misted up like the devil on the windows, and it wasn't easy to get rid of it, because so few of the windows would open.

"What are you laughing at?"

"I was thinking of the house you're working on. You arrive there and the first thing you do is tear down what little was already done. And then you take away a pair of taps. As if it didn't matter in the least. If anyone comes back while you're here it'll look worse than it did before. They'll think there's been some kind of *vandalism* going on."

"It had to be re-done, for God's sake."

"Yes, of course. But just think if someone comes while you're out here."

"Well, I've got everything down, crystal-clear. On paper. Look here!" (And he took it carefully out of his breast pocket.)

Credit:

Two returned taps, Poggenpohl brand	1230.00
(Uppsala Builders' Merchants)	

Debit:

Tile cement, Väärtilä, 4 tubs @ 35.90	143.60
4 tubs grey grouting @ 24.90	99.60
Various tools and equipment	470.00
To be repaid to contractor	516.80

Torsten had written everything down crystal-clear in a few seconds on the back of a wine and spirits list, torn off the page and stuffed it into his wallet. Nobody could accuse him of improprieties in business.

"So you can see that if these people have any sense they'll soon realise that I've acted in their best interests. And it's easy enough to put the taps back on again. The main thing must surely be that something gets done?"

"Yes, sure."

"Why are you laughing?"

"It's so like you. You've always been like that."

"You think so?"

"Yes, of course I do. You were always wild as a boy. Whatever you were making, rabbit hutches or snow-shovels or whatever, it always had to be taken to pieces and re-done in a different way."

"Really? I don't remember that at all."

"Well, that's how it was."

They had to wait for a long time at the red lights just beyond the Stockholm roundabout. Heavy lorries trundled in and out of timber merchants and repair shops built in the most simple and utilitarian style in the world. A few wet moped riders were battling through against the rain.

"It's mad what they've built out here."

"You were a bit *odd*, you were. As a boy. You were like your uncle, the sheet metalworker. He was really funny too. There were a lot of stories going round about him."

"Really? I can't remember that at all," Torsten repeated, not entirely honestly.

The lights turned green, and Torsten – who had kept the worn-out old engine on high revs so that it wouldn't stop in the rain – managed to get the jalopy going again by easing the clutch in gradually.

It was strange: although they should have had so much to talk about, neither of them was particularly communicative.

"But you must remember the funniest one of all, when he was going to repair the church steeple at Berg."

"No. I can't remember that. Tell me."

A taxi swerved in only a fraction in front of Torsten's wing, and he cursed the cheek of the drivers of today. He could feel that his car really was worn out: it didn't steer properly as it used to. What luck that he hadn't had to carry tiles in it! There was dense traffic and bad visibility, which meant a slow and frustrating drive. That was fine by Torsten. He wanted a little more time to talk to this man, the last link uniting him with his own childhood. The question was how he was going to get anything sensible out of him.

"Berg church has an unusual spire. Tall and steep. About

51

a hundred feet high. And it looks higher because the church is up on a ridge. Some time around 1924 the copper plate on the spire needed renewing. The parish council was as stingy as hell. In the end it was only Clason whose estimate was low enough to get the contract. And Clason, mean as he was, did the whole thing as a one-man job. Put up scaffolding and lowered the old sheeting and hoisted the new. Bloody dangerous, of course, but he was as stubborn as he was mean. So naturally, he managed it. Hard of hearing and obstinate and absorbed in his work, he hung high up there in his cradle hammering in his nails in sunshine and rain, sweating and swearing and hammering so that it could be heard over the whole district. It took weeks, of course – no, it took months. But nobody was much bothered about that. The main thing was that it was being done. The local people came and went, and on hot spring days there were some who felt sympathy for poor old Clason hanging and hammering up there, with a bottle of water in his belt and sweat running down his brow that he couldn't even wipe off, for fear of dropping the hammer on their skulls."

"Ye-es," said Torsten, tentatively. "No one can really escape his destiny."

"Do you think so? I don't think so at all. I think everything comes from within. I think people decide for themselves who they're going to be. Anyway, there's Clason hanging there one fine day, when the vicar himself comes walking along. He looks up and sees the metalworker hanging up there like an outsize fly on the shining copper plating, hammering and swearing as usual. It's possible that the vicar felt a kind of prick of bad conscience. Because, let's face it, he'd been at all the meetings of the parish council where they'd discussed every possible way of dealing with the problem. And brushed them aside because they were too expensive.

"Anyway, the vicar is standing there staring up at the ball and the cross and the golden weathercock on the top of Berg church, and trying to make this strange hanging and hammering man hear him. 'Clason!' he yells with his authoritative voice. But the man up there doesn't seem to hear. The vicar shouts again, and finally Clason begins to get an idea that the small black figure down there with the red face set in a white collar probably wants him for something.

"So Clason, angry as hell of course at having to interrupt his work and lower himself down, a long and difficult job when you don't have any helper, finally lands at the vicar's feet. 'Good morning, Clason!' 'Good morning, vicar!' And there they stand looking at each other – no, staring at each other – in the hope that one of them at least will think of something to say.

"The vicar, who's by profession, so to speak, a little more talkative, comes to himself first and says:

"'Aren't you frightened, Clason, all alone and so high up?'

"'*What's that?*' says Clason. (He must have been only about twenty-five, but was already hard of hearing from all the hammering. You remember he was completely stone-deaf when you and your mother moved in with him, but it must have already begun then.) So Clason looks him straight in the face, wipes the sweat from his brow and says: 'What's that?'

"'Aren't you frightened when you're on your own so high up?'

"Clason stares back, thinks to himself long and hard, spits out his quid of tobacco that he's had with him all the time up there, and says:

"'I can tell you, vicar, that I'm never frightened, not even if I'm so high *that I can hear the angels fart!*'"

"Well. Very interesting," said Torsten, and started off with a sudden rush at the next set of traffic lights.

"Listen," said Stig, unconcerned. "I've got an idea. Let's drive past the liquor store and buy a bottle of aquavit and some bread and sausage to set ourselves up for a good while longer, and then I'll come on out with you and we'll get things finished. I don't feel as if I want to sit at home staring at the television screen all afternoon."

"Have you got some cash, then?"

"Hell, yes," said Stig, "we'll manage."

As they were parking, which was difficult because the street was more or less blocked by a man on crutches of about their own age getting out of a taxi (there was a devil of a hooting the whole length of the street and an old woman was complaining in a loud voice about people on sickness benefit getting a free taxi to the liquor store), Torsten took the opportunity, rather cautiously and diffidently it must be said, to ask Stig:

"I say, is it true that you've been a preacher, too?"

"As sure as hell I have. But it wasn't for very long. So it doesn't count. You know that my mother went a lot to the Lutheran Missionary Society. So I went on a course for a while. I think the idea was that I should become a missionary. But things didn't actually get that far. But as sure as hell I've been a preacher. Better to ask what I haven't been. I travelled round for a while giving lectures about vegetarianism. And selling cabbage and books about eating raw vegetables. There's hardly a city or small town where I didn't give vegetarian lectures in the forties. It's just that I've kind of always found it very easy to convince other people about things. But it's never been so easy to convince myself. And I also went in for Esperanto at one time, by the way. Esperanto and vegetarianism were sort of once my ideals. Raw vegetables would make people healthy and when everyone spoke Esperanto there wouldn't be any more wars. But that's a long time ago now. I don't really believe in it any more."

They squeezed into the shop where the afternoon queues had just started to form. Torsten had the feeling that everything was going to brighten up now.

"Well, as I said," said Torsten, "I've got my business in crystal-clear order. That I have."

The queue was moving slowly and tediously ahead of them. Thank God there was no one there asking for special brands, anyway.

"I heard you."

"Crystal-clear, as I said," repeated Torsten. "If there are any mistakes, at least they aren't in my accounts.

"As I said," Torsten went on. "But there might be something in the fact that it isn't always easy to put things in order. I can't remember any time when my own affairs were well-ordered, so to speak. There was always something wrong. It was all right when I was working at Ekeby. There was so much money in the fifties. That was when I got enough to buy the house. And the car. The fifties were good in their way. People listened to wireless programmes and drove around in their cars on Sundays. But first I had to lose the boy, of course. He was a good, decent boy: I had great hopes for him. But then he had to get in with those characters with their motorbikes. And things happened as they did."

"Dreadful," said Stig.

"Yes, it *was* dreadful. The wife was never the same again after that. She sort of lost herself. She'd go around doing her chores as before. But she wasn't really there. Do you understand what I mean?"

"You *can* lose yourself. I've seen other people do it."

"It became extremely peculiar after a while. It was a bit like talking to a goldfish."

"Did you know that you can't have goldfish together with other fish in an aquarium?"

"No, I didn't know that."

"They give off ammonia through their gills. And it's too much for the other fish."

"Well, I had no idea."

"That's the way it is."

"Shall we take three bottles so that we have a little in reserve?"

"Can we afford it?"

"Yes, we damned well can. I said my accounts are in crystal-clear order."

We must imagine Sisyphus happy

"YES, it looks bloody awful here," said Stig.

There was some truth in that.

The house was as empty as when Torsten had left it. Somewhere, it was hard to say where, a window was banging in the wind on the upper floor. That was rather strange, because Torsten couldn't recall having heard that particular noise before. But the wind had freshened up a bit since it had begun to clear. Now, when he had a visitor, so to speak, the bathroom did look rather dreadful, with everything he'd hacked off the walls lying in fragments all over the floor. And it undeniably did look a bit bare with the taps taken out. He couldn't really understand how the job could have seemed to be so easy when he first came in.

"Let's see if we can clear out this rubbish," said Stig. "You can't move here without risking a broken leg. Is there a wheelbarrow and a spade anywhere?"

"No," said Torsten. "I wondered that myself, but I didn't manage to find anything."

"There's no point in having a drink before we've put this in order. You could take the bucket and get started on mixing the tile cement and I'll see about clearing this lot out."

Stig had disappeared before Torsten even had time to ask him how the hell he was going to solve that problem. And he realised that he'd have to go over to the kitchen now to put some water in the bucket. He couldn't help noticing that his feet had left quite distinct marks here and there. But that didn't matter very much. It was pretty obvious that it would all have to be cleaned up anyway if tiles were to be laid. He'd worked in a house once on a similar job where the lady had always made him take off his boots every time he came in. He remembered that with a certain annoyance. It had been somewhere out in Bergsbrunna, and it had almost driven him mad because he kept having to go out for materials all the time. Shoes on, shoes off! In the end he could have throttled the old bag. But you didn't do that sort of thing.

So now, he hoped, he had everything he needed. Tile cement and grouting. If he could only find something to mix it with, all would be well. Carrying in the tiles and getting the metal bands off the bundles would be a troublesome job; he'd already got breathless out at the builders' merchants. It would probably be best to wait for Stig. How on earth could he have been a preacher! And then all that about vegetarian lectures! The question was whether he was an entirely reliable person, or one of those rogues who take pleasure in spinning other people yarns.

Torsten stirred the cement briskly with a broom-handle he hadn't even bothered to take off the broom, and let the water in the kitchen sink flow over and down on to his mix in a fine and well-judged stream. It had to have exactly the right consistency. He still had this sort of thing at his fingertips, and he felt a moment's pleasure in his own skill. He turned off the kitchen tap and immediately heard weird noises inside the building, noises that made him jump. He remembered the closed door and the strange card with Sophie K. written on it. Surely things couldn't be happening up there again?

And it would be too much to hope that the contractor had finally put in an appearance to get on with the job he'd left.

Well, whatever it was, it was time for Torsten to set to work again. Anything was possible in this damned house.

But coming out of the bathroom, what does he find but Stig cheerfully shovelling broken tiles and dust into a fine old-fashioned wheelbarrow with a good strong shovel. And another shovel is standing leaning against the wheelbarrow.

"Hi! Come and lend a hand! I've put the aquavit and the sausage in the fridge. We'll have a drop when we've got rid of the rubbish. Great that you got the tile cement ready."

"Where the hell did you get the barrow and the shovels?"

"Nothing hard about that. I called on our neighbour. Nice fellow. Pensioner. His name's Tage Petterson and he used to be a clerk for the Gas Board. He can't see too well now. So he doesn't use his tools very often. But he had everything in damned fine order. Really decent toolshed. Of course, you can see that nothing much has been done to the garden for a while. And his wife's in hospital. She's apparently been there for some time."

"Well, well."

"And he was extremely surprised, by the way, to hear that we're here working. He says he hasn't seen a single person here since the early summer. There must have been something wrong with the planning permission. And Petterson was quite certain that the owner lives in Stockholm. But he's gone bankrupt and disappeared. He was one of those property speculators, you know. He'll be in Majorca now, or the Bahamas or whatever it's called. Petterson said he was pleased to see things moving again here. The idea was to have the whole thing renovated last summer. It was going to be a posh family house. When he came here there were four different families living in it, with masses of children. And then it apparently stood empty for a while."

"Well, well. Amazing."

"Yes. It's never good when things stand still. If you're not moving, you're going downhill, my mother used to say."

"Well, it's only us moving in it now."

"Will you take the other shovel so that we get rid of all this crap before it's time for a bite of sausage and a drink?"

Torsten was coughing violently in the cloud of dust they were throwing up. The wheelbarrow was heavy and it wasn't very easy getting it over the threshold. Where the devil should he put the rubbish? He found a corner by the box that must have held the fridge-freezer, and tipped the broken tiles out on the wet mud. He could hardly stop coughing. Nevertheless he couldn't help noticing that the weather had brightened up. From the gloomiest November it had turned into early October again; air as clear as it can only be on certain days in autumn in Uppsala. There were still isolated leaves hanging here and there in the trees, looking like gold coins. They took alternate barrow-loads, and it was six altogether, six barrows piled high. It's incredible how much there is as soon as you hack it down. It was light work for Stig. Heavy for Torsten. But he recovered pretty quickly when the aquavit went down. It spread right out to the most sensitive parts of his being and made his heart beat more easily.

They drank out of Torsten's two Thermos flask lids. They weren't very well washed up, but on the other hand they gave pretty decent measures.

"Sausage," said Torsten.

"Yes," said Stig. "If it hadn't been for that damned Balk, I could probably have been in Majorca or the Bahamas right now too."

"Who's Balk?"

"No, obviously you wouldn't know who Balk is. And that's probably just as well. But he did me a great wrong."

"So it sounds," said Torsten.

"I once had a haulage business with three lorries," said Stig. "It was a devil of a job, but good fun too. And I earned a lot of money. And then I almost got a wife who was going to inherit two big gravel pits at Åsen near Surahammar. Gravel pits like that were worth millions even then, at the end of the fifties. You know what sand and gravel cost in those days, when they were building so much all over the place. I remember Balk taking me up to the edge of the biggest gravel pit once, so close to the edge that the sand nearly started giving way under us, and he said: 'This gravel pit is worth millions.' I remember him saying it."

"So who was Balk, then?"

"A devil, a really evil man. I carried gravel for him. From his bloody gravel pit. And I liked his daughter a lot. She was a fine girl."

"And you weren't allowed to marry his daughter?"

"No. Though it wasn't as simple as that. Do you think I'd have let Balk decide a thing like that for me? What was that funny noise, by the way?"

"I didn't hear anything."

"I thought it sounded as if someone was going up the stairs."

"I've checked. There's no one living up there."

"What's up there, then?"

"Just a locked door. To an old flat that they haven't renovated. And there's a card on the door."

"What's on it?"

"Sophie K."

"Are you sure there's no one living there, then?"

"You said yourself that that bloke Petterson said there hadn't been a single person here since June. If you don't believe me, you'd better go and check for yourself. I'll go and start some tiling now. What's the time?"

"Quarter past three."

"Bloody hell. Almost the whole day gone and not a single tile put up. And never a sign of the devil who's going to sort out the money for me. You go up and look. I'll make a start again, so that at least one of us gets something done."

Stig disappeared up the stairs. Torsten tightened the cord to mark the first row and set to work. The light could have been better, but anyway it was a relief finally – even so late in the day – to get going on what he'd actually come here to do. Life certainly had some strange and messy sides to it.

Torsten had the feeling of being a fairly contented fly moving up a wall. A wall that was the back of something. The back of something else, he could imagine to himself, that was the front.

He's made the whole thing up

STIG TOOK HIS TIME. He was presumably making a systematic investigation of everything that was up there. That's good, Torsten thought. Then I'll at least be able to get a bit of work done in peace. Perhaps he won't even come back at all. You never know. I think there's something a little odd about Stig. There's something he's holding back. And then those gravel pits! Worth millions! That he'd never owned! What imaginings! He's made the whole thing up. Did he use to make things up as a little boy?

It was the devil's own job for Torsten to remember. Suddenly he couldn't remember a single episode at all from his childhood that Stig had been present in.

When they used to cycle to Sätra Spring in the summertime? But Stig wasn't one of the ones who cycled there, was he? Or when they used to cycle along the canal and torment the lock-keepers? Torsten could remember a number of faces, but not Stig's. And yet he was certain there was some interesting event that Stig had taken part in. There must be one.

It's actually amazing what strangers these childhood friends seem when you meet them again. And they profess to have a level of friendship that in reality they can hardly claim.

Torsten was now so high up the wall that he had to find something to stand on. It was the devil's own job to reach up to the top edge. He was really quite short, and had quite often been the butt of ridicule on that account. He went off to look in wardrobes and cupboards throughout the whole flat in the hope of finding a step-ladder or at least a box to stand on.

He went angrily from door to door, opening and closing them. All he could actually find were a few discarded bits of piping at the bottom of a cupboard. Two empty half-bottles that some earlier craftsman had left behind. Then just at the very moment when he practically fell over the three-legged stool that had been standing right before his eyes the whole time in the living room, he remembered Irene.

Irene was a memory that he didn't often go back to, because he wanted to keep it exactly as it was. And the memory of Irene was associated with this whole idea of being slightly too short. One of his memories was of standing with Irene, one winter evening – it must have been at the beginning of the thirties – waiting for the doors of the cinema to open. Hand in hand. They often used to take off their woollen gloves to be able to hold each other's hand. And that uncomfortable feeling of standing in a crowd where almost everyone was taller than yourself. And then the doors of paradise would open. The smell of dust, discarded toffee-wrappers, the odour of wet wool from overcoats that had been snowed on. Paradise lay not so much in what was showing on the white screen, all the sentimental dreaming with Clark Gable and Ava Gardner and whatever their names were, but more in all that he could do with Irene in there in the dark. And they weren't little things, either. All the warm and soft, even warm and damp, surfaces and crevices you could explore. In the middle of *The Thief of Bagdad*, starring Douglas Fairbanks, he had proudly witnessed himself giving this passionate little girl an orgasm just with his fingers, and so powerful a one that she could hardly stay sitting in her seat.

To be able to touch Irene – to touch her softer, more intimate parts – it was virtually essential to go to the cinema. Outside there was nothing but snow piling up, and his house was out of the question. He was still living at home with his mother. He had the bedroom and his mother slept on the sofa downstairs by that time. And he'd set up his photographic darkroom in the attic. But taking girls home wasn't even a possibility.

A time of dreams, a dreamy time. And associated with constant snowfall, woollen gloves, Irene's worn-out winter coat, snowflakes settling on her hair.

She lived with two old ladies in quite a big house. The ladies were her aunts and they were very well-to-do. They were the daughters of a dean, and didn't mix with just anybody. Torsten had seen them a number of times out in Hallstahammar, but he'd hardly ever talked to them since the church ecumenical meeting where the parcel auction had been held and where he'd met Irene. Occasions like that brought about brief meetings between the well-to-do and the less well-to-do in Hallstahammar. Before Jesus they were for a while all equal, so to speak.

They used to meet a good way from the house on the corner by Knektbacken Hill. They also had to think up quite complicated white lies for Irene to explain why she was out in the evenings. It's true that she was nineteen years old, but as far as the cinema and things like that were concerned, it didn't help a bit. Hadn't they almost threatened to throw her out when a girl friend cut her hair short?

The next autumn Irene had disappeared from his life almost as unexpectedly as she'd come into it. She'd been sent to a school in Uppsala to study domestic science. They'd said that they'd write letters to each other, but that didn't last long.

But years afterwards she would still appear in his dreams.

And always in winter when it was snowing. She was a sort of opening for him, an opening to another, warmer world which he'd never quite dared to think of staying in. It was as if it wasn't for him.

It's strange, Torsten said to himself, that I'm having so many peculiar thoughts today. Some really unpleasant, and some rather nice ones.

Things are coming back to me that I haven't thought of for years.

It's as if this strange house had some kind of influence on how you think. I'll go out to the kitchen soon and have another drop. But just look at how well the tiles are coming along! Neat and tidy rows, beautiful Finnish tiles. And wait till I've done the grouting. With just the right light-grey grouting that'll go so well with the blue.

It really is splendid when you can bring a little order into life. Even if you know that one fine day someone will come along and tear everything down again and replace it with something else. One single moment is good, and that's when you see it getting into shape, almost of its own accord.

"It's damned strange up there on the top floor, I can tell you."

Stig turned up behind him so suddenly that he jumped. He couldn't understand how he'd managed to come back in such complete silence. Obviously Torsten hadn't had ears or eyes for anything other than his tiles.

"It looks pretty good here. It's coming on well. Blue looks good."

"What's so strange up there? It's locked."

"Not so well locked that you can't pick it open with a penknife. Come and see."

66

It was only with reluctance that Torsten climbed down from his stool. He was so much into his work now that he was unwilling to interrupt it. He hoped that Stig hadn't found anything really unpleasant, something that might spoil the whole working atmosphere for him. Perhaps there was a corpse up there? Perhaps Sophie K. was dead? Murdered perhaps? And perhaps in that case the murderer would come back to discover that Stiggsy and Torsten knew of the secret. Torsten's heart began to beat very hard and fast. As a matter of fact his heart hadn't been good the whole day, and working like a slave for the last hour with aquavit in his system hadn't made it any better.

But he had no desire to let Stig see that he was frightened, either.

"I'll come with you," Torsten said. "But I really haven't got time now for so many distractions. It's already late in the day and I've got masses to finish off here."

Stig had indeed managed to pick the lock of Sophie K.'s door with a penknife; it was the old-fashioned, very simple but reliable type. Torsten had picked many a lock in the same way when he was a boy. It was just a matter of getting the knife in far enough to be able to exert pressure and force the bolt to slide back.

The door creaked and groaned noisily, and Torsten hoped that no one was standing down there in the stairway right now listening to them – it's remarkable how soon a guilty conscience begins to prick.

But there was nothing sensational up here. The room that opened up in front of them was narrow and almost empty. The old-fashioned brown wallpaper made the whole impression even more melancholy. A pair of old brown curtains hung at the window. Against one wall was an office desk of the roll-top kind, and there was a swivel-chair at the desk.

Whoever had been living here last seemed to have been using the room more as an office than a living room. Torsten didn't like being in here. For the first time that day he had a feeling of being involved in something illicit. And it was Stig who'd dragged him into it. He longed to get back to his wall, to his tile cement and his vague dreams about a winter long ago. There was absolutely nothing productive that could be done up here.

"What's so special about this, then?" he said, rather angrily. "Did you really need to drag me up here to look at an old office?"

"But look here, then," said Stiggsy, opening a door that Torsten hadn't paid any attention to.

"Yes, that's probably the old kitchen."

It was indeed a kitchen, or perhaps cooking corner would be a better description. The cupboard painted in a 1930s cheerless pea-green colour and, on the floor, worn-out cork mats. It must have been ages since anyone had washed up in this sink. The whole thing wasn't so different from his mother's old kitchen at home in Hallstahammar. There was even a kitchen table still here. Stiggsy pointed in silence to a big bulky object that could just be made out in the half-light under the kitchen table.

"It's a safe," Stiggsy said.

Torsten stepped nearer in disbelief. It was a real solid old safe of the smaller type. A metal plate proclaimed the makers as Ekwall Brothers of Gothenburg – a very long time ago by the look of it. It was very dusty but otherwise seemed undamaged, and the door, which had a proper wheel that obviously had to be turned in particular combinations to open it, was firmly closed. That was only to be expected. No one would leave a safe open.

"So I see," said Torsten.

"But don't you realise, there could be absolutely anything in it!"

"Not fish, for instance. You'd know that by the smell."

"No, but money. You never know what can happen nowadays. With all the drug dealers and strange goings-on."

"There's nothing odd about an old safe being left here. Especially since it looks as if it was an office up here. They're not easy to move."

"It might be stolen!"

"Why should anyone steal it and put it up here without even trying to open it?"

"Shouldn't we try to open it?"

"You're mad. Then it'll be you who's trying to steal it." Stiggsy became rather thoughtful.

"Perhaps thieves are intending to come back and open it."

"Well, if that happens it won't be so funny for us."

"We could try dragging it out from under the table and tilting it about a bit to see if we can hear anything inside it."

This temptation was one that even Torsten found all too enticing. It was just that although the damned safe could certainly be dragged out from under the table – leaving deep gouges in the linoleum – managing to do anything like moving it about was nowhere near so easy.

With a cold sweat breaking out on his brow, Torsten managed to tilt the safe slightly. It definitely sounded as if something slid across the bottom, but it was more like a single metal object than the promising bundles of notes that Stig had probably imagined were there.

"It must be the key," said Stig.

"But they surely can't have been so bloody stupid as to lock the key inside!

"Anyway, it can't be a key, you fool: it's a combination lock."

69

"No, it isn't. Can't you see, there's a keyhole underneath!"

"It doesn't much matter, if we don't know the combination."

Torsten wiped the sweat off his brow.

"Listen, I don't think we'd be particularly good, either of us, at safe-breaking. Wouldn't it be just as well if we put the damned thing back where it was before there's hell to pay if someone comes?"

Stiggsy went along with that, it seemed. But he cast longing glances back at the room with the strange safe as Torsten carefully pulled the door to. The sun had given way to cloud again, or could it be dusk already falling?

"Listen, I think we should have another drop, and then I'm going to carry on with the walls anyway so that I get away from here before nine o'clock tonight. But I don't see how the hell I'll be able to sort out the finances if no one ever comes that I can speak to."

"You could send in your bill by post."

"Where to, though?"

"Well, there's always some damned place."

"I'll have to ring up Pentti, the Finn, and talk to him. He must know."

"If there'd been a million or so in that safe you wouldn't have needed to talk to him."

"No – that's true. Of course. But things like that don't happen in real life. Would you like some more sausage? And what would you have done with a million if you'd found it?"

Stiggsy looked a bit uncertain.

"Would you have started your own business? Again? And had taxes to pay and the authorities chasing you and trade unions and forms to fill in and all the bloody lot?"

"I think I'm too old for that," Stiggsy said.

"Or moved to Spain, perhaps. Sitting drinking plonk and

staring at a beach where you don't want to swim because you already know what it feels like? No, it's a bit too late for us."

Stiggsy went quieter.

"That million is just something you dream about to avoid facing up to the fact that things aren't going to change very much. You only need to be afraid of old age and death if you're sure that everything will soon be happier and more interesting than it is now. If you don't find that million you'll die a lot more easily."

Stiggsy didn't seem in the least convinced.

"At any rate, I could have bought a new car instead of the old banger I've got now," he said gloomily. "Not even getting through its test today!"

"Yes, you could always have done that."

At last Torsten was able to turn to his bucket of tile cement. He was glad to see it hadn't yet set completely.

I'll never get Balk off my mind

THINGS WERE GOING more slowly now. For some reason. Perhaps it was because he had to get down from the stool every single time to pick up a new tile and put the cement on it. If there'd been a scaffold here he could have done several at each go. But there was Stig. He ought to be able to help. It isn't so particularly difficult to learn how much cement to put on a tile.

"Come and help me, Stiggsy."

"OK."

"You see how much you have to put on?"

"OK."

"Why do you say 'OK' all the time?"

"We used to say that in America."

"I see."

"If I found a million in an old safe, I'd buy a haulage business again. Haulage is the best, you know."

"Do you think you can get them for a million crowns nowadays?"

"If Balk hadn't got in the way, I'd have a haulage business worth several million by now."

"How did he get in the way, then?"

Stig seemed at first not to have heard the question. He had a method of putting the cement on the tile that looked as if he was spreading butter on sandwiches, and it was slightly irritating. But Torsten decided not to say anything about that.

"I should have shot him, the bastard! Shooting him would have been the right thing to do!"

"But what did he do, then, that was so awful?"

"Just after the war – no, it must have been at the beginning of the fifties – I started driving a lorry for an old boy in Lisjö who had a haulage business. Driving was something I'd learned in the army. This old boy in Lisjö, whose name was Ivarsson by the way, did a lot of driving for the building trade, and there was a lot of that kind of work then, at the beginning of the fifties; and we did a bit of driving for the brewery in Ramnäs when their own driver couldn't cope in the summer. But mostly it was sand and gravel for the building trade. There was such a helluva lot of building sites on the go then, especially around Västerås, so we were driving almost day and night sometimes. And it wasn't always very easy. The roads weren't exactly as good as they are now.

"Balk was a devil.

"Balk did me a lot of harm.

"Balk was the right name for him. He had the knack of balking you at every turn.

"He had a particular way of looking at you as if everything you suggested was ridiculous. If he realised that something was important to you, like for example his little Elin, his daughter, a kind, shy girl who kept herself mostly to the kitchen, because Balk detested going out to the kitchen – well, then he'd become even more of a swine.

"He would think up long and peculiar stories to prevent you meeting her. If she hadn't got measles, then it would be something about her having had to go to look after an old lady in Lisjö. I could see her, in her white dress with the blue dots, walking along between the raspberry bushes as we spoke, she was so close that she could probably hear what he was saying. Believe me, that didn't bother him in the least. On the contrary, he enjoyed it, the sod. He was one of those people who enjoy being able to wind you round their little finger."

"You should have stood up for yourself."

"Of course I should. That was the worst of it, that I couldn't assert myself. I've actually never been able to assert myself, that's the worst thing about me. So I just stand there like an idiot and clench my fists in my trouser pockets. And imagine all the firm and decisive and definite things I'm going to do. But none of it gets done.

"She asked me to take her away from there. And I often thought about it, but somehow it never happened.

"Then, when that bastard Balk sees he's not getting any-where with me, and not with her either for that matter, he suggests to me we should become partners. Haulage was a good business in those days; as I said, it was in the middle of the building boom. So he buys another lorry and we get going. Then when it's starting to go well, the bastard slings me out and takes everything from me. Wife and haulage business and the whole bloody lot."

"But how could he?"

"Well, that's a bloody long story. First he turned Elin against me. The bastard pulled me to pieces, told her that I drank too much. Of course I drank a bit, but who the hell didn't? Anyway there were no driving accidents, so no prob-lems. I drank a bit. But that swine went and talked to the Temperance Board, set the authorities on to me, made sure they took my driving licence away."

"And Elin?"

"Hell only knows what got into her. She was used to obey-ing. So she simply obeyed. She had no will of her own. I let her go. Yes, I let everything go."

"Was it then you went to America?"

"Yes, that was when I went to America. I stopped drinking. Imagine that. I really stopped drinking. And started preaching and got in with the Pentecostalists. It was actually quite a happy time, I can tell you. Though of course I didn't feel as if I was properly myself. Not often, anyway. But listen, Torsten, I'd really like to know what you'd say: Do you think that there are people who are evil?"

"Well, it depends. If you think of Hitler and Stalin . . ."

"I don't give a shit about Hitler and Stalin. They're dead, both of them. Are there or aren't there?"

"What?"

"Evil people, like I said."

"Doesn't it depend a bit on what you mean?"

"Believe me. There are evil people. You think I've got hung up on this man Balk, don't you? That things might look different from his point of view. I promise you there's no such thing as Balk's point of view. But if you don't want us to talk about Balk, we can easily go on to something else. The truth is that there's no shortage of evil people. Just listen to this and you'll see what I mean:

"A few times a year around about that time, I would drive over to the hospital in Tystberga. Food and milk and things like that. All stuff for the kitchens, and I usually had to carry it in on my own.

"It was a hospital for the mentally ill.

"It wasn't often anyone went there, except for the ones who belonged there. They were people who couldn't leave: people who'd been weak in the head since childhood, idiots who couldn't look after themselves. Some defective from birth and others very old and no longer conscious of where they were or who they were. They would sit in the corridors or move around slowly from room to room like cattle.

"I think it was extremely rare for them ever to have a visit from relatives. I never saw any of them, anyway. These were people they'd got rid of, that the whole world had got rid of. And they didn't know any other world.

"The shameful thing, though, was the way the nurses treated them. They had some kind of coffee break in the afternoons, and this coffee was extremely important to most of them. It was hot and black and sweet. The sugar bowl especially was important to them.

"But the sugar was carefully rationed. They couldn't just take it any old how. Oh, no. And to get an extra bit, the poor feeble-minded souls had to perform tricks that the nurses thought up. Jumping over a stick that they held higher and higher. Balancing it on their noses. You know, they treated these people exactly like dogs. And they didn't feel a moment's shame. They laughed when they saw me watching, and they tried to outdo one another in this shocking spectacle just because I was there.

"Tears came to my eyes, but as usual I couldn't assert myself. I couldn't just sit there, either. I couldn't do any-thing.

"Evil people are quite ordinary people, aren't they? There's nothing strange or special about them. Everyone always tries to find something special in evil people. They're *sick* or *perverted* or something like that. But it's not like that! It's as if all the time everyone was hiding and denying something that they knew full well.

"Hell, sometimes I believe that I actually killed the old man. But that's probably just something I imagined. I knocked him off the edge of his own gravel-pit so many times in my mind, and saw his disgusting hand as the last thing sticking up out of the sand, that I sometimes believe that I actually did it. Don't you believe that I did?"

Torsten was silent for a long time. Then he said, thoughtfully:

"No. I don't believe it at all."

He turned and went out to the kitchen with determined steps and opened the door of the fridge. It was of course just as he'd thought. No bottles there. I wonder what he's done with the empties. He'll have hidden the last one, of course. He'll obviously have done that. He hides the last one the way dogs hide bones. And I'm not going to run around looking for it.

There was a bit of the sausage left, though. Torsten held it in his hand and began to chew on it meditatively. It wasn't very good sausage, but sausage was seldom any good nowadays.

That was just what I expected. While I took just a drop, or possibly a couple of small ones, that sly guy has been quietly drinking the rest. It was a mistake to bring him here with me. All he does is spin yarns about himself the whole time. If I'd said what I *really* thought, it would have been that neither the old man nor the girl had ever existed. Gravel-pits worth millions! Ridiculous! And the haulage firm – like hell! He's never owned a lorry in his life. He's made the whole thing up to have something to blame. There's such a helluva lot of *bitterness* in him. You have to watch out for the bitter ones. They're contagious. Life is full of losers, who've only got that way because they want to be defeated. It's as if they couldn't get by without being defeated. There's a wall of tiles in this bloody ghost-house now that wasn't here yesterday, for instance. I'll soon have it finished and I've set them straight and neat. There isn't a luxury hotel anywhere that wouldn't be pleased to have a wall like that in its lavatories.

I don't know whether I'll ever get paid for my work. I don't even know whether it'll be me who finishes the work off. And

I don't know who I've done it for or whether anyone will appreciate it. Perhaps the people who come to live here won't like the colour. Perhaps they'd have liked small tiles better: as people did in the fifties. But at least I've achieved something in the real world.

"Hey, there's water on the floor now. There's a leak somewhere," said Stig. "There's a lot more water here than there was a while ago."

"Oh, hell, I thought I'd turned it off. You could take this rag and mop up a bit."

Stig's attempts at mopping up didn't appear to be particularly energetic. It seemed as if he was running out of steam. But of course it wasn't a very good rag he had, either. It certainly wasn't much of a helper he'd got on this occasion. Torsten went out to the kitchen again. His shoes left real footprints this time, but he didn't give a damn. He bent down under the main inlet to the dishwasher. It must be the main inlet after all. His pipe-wrench was lying where he'd left it. He pulled so hard that the cold sweat broke out again on his forehead, but there was nothing left to tighten on the tap. It was as tight as it would go. It must have been the water left in the pipe, he reassured himself.

Through the kitchen window he could see a red kite hanging high over the tree tops and almost entirely motionless in the wind. It's nice to think about something else from time to time. Torsten had also once had a red kite. He'd made it himself, and on his very first attempt to fly it, it had caught in one of the tall maple trees on Knektbacken Hill at Hallstahammar. He'd struggled with it for a whole afternoon, to the unconcealed delight of the boys next door, with long sticks, with stones (meant to hit the kite and knock it down, but which of course kept landing in the most unlikely places instead), but the kite stayed hanging where it was. He could still see it hanging there the next winter, torn to ribbons and in a sorry state at the top of the tree, when he was too old to play with kites any more (and had already begun working in the grocery shop that faced on to the street in Clason's house). Like a stranded bird. What was so great about kites was that you could be in two places at once. Down on the ground and high up there. You could look down on yourself, and you were just an upturned face, a little pink speck holding on in some strange way to the slender cord.

No, the whole thing's a pack of lies, Torsten said to himself once again.

Just at that moment there was a ring at the door. It was a sound that boded no good.

A strange interlude

THE RINGING at the door went on and on. Whoever it was standing out there, it must be someone who wanted something very badly.

Stiggsy was nowhere to be found. It was difficult to rid yourself of a certain suspicion: he must be upstairs on the top floor shaking that old safe about again, of course. Is there any limit to the childish hopes and expectations people make for themselves? Or had he just lain down to sleep in some quiet corner? All this talk about Balk was obviously something to do with the drink.

Torsten Bergman still held the sopping wet rag which he'd equally unsuccessfully used to mop up the worst of the water from the bathroom floor. It looked as if the flow of water was more, rather than less, now. And why that person just stood out there ringing, instead of trying the door and finding that it was unlocked as usual was completely unintelligible to him.

A range of unpleasant possibilities passed through Torsten's mind as he went to open the door. But it turned out to be nothing like he'd imagined.

In the doorway stood a well-built, sandy-haired woman holding a crying child on her arm and another by the hand; they must have been about two and five years old. Torsten wasn't so good at guessing the age of little children any more. Her blue dress, which looked quite pretty and well-ironed, had short sleeves. Her muscular arms were covered in freckles. What the devil could this woman want? She seemed to be very keen to come into the house for some reason and Torsten was too surprised even to wonder why. He held the door open politely for her, and she didn't hesitate for a moment before coming in.

"Yes?"

She looked around in the hall and took a few steps into the living room, fast steps as if she was running away from something or somebody. Then she looked Torsten straight in the eyes – her eyes were pale blue and rather hard.

"Telephone?"

"No. There isn't a phone here. Things haven't got that far yet. It'll be a while before a phone's put in here. If one ever is."

"But I need a phone. It's urgent."

We'll have to hope it's not a trick, Torsten thought. There apparently are people who get into old people's houses on some such pretext and then rob them. But there's damn all to steal here. There should be a bottle in the fridge, but even that's gone. There's nothing movable to steal here. And if she thinks she can rob me she's fooling herself, that's for sure. And that damned water's still dripping in the bathroom. How can I get rid of her? And how long will it be before the water's over the threshold?

"But we haven't got a telephone here."

"I must get to a phone. I must talk to my husband."

Instead of explaining, the woman put the two-year-old down on the now dirty and only partly paper-covered parquet flooring. She let go of the elder child, who quickly hid behind her back. Where the hell was Stiggsy?

Perhaps she has the cops after her? Torsten tried to remember, rather vaguely, the evening-paper placard headlines about foreigners, refugees, hiding from the police in churches and houses. Or could it be that her husband was after her? Perhaps he'd turn up at any minute and create a helluva scene? Perhaps he ought to look a bit friendly. He tried to tempt the little boy out from behind his mother's back by beckoning with his hand – the mother's hips were quite magnificent – but the child preferred to stay hidden.

"No," said Torsten, "unfortunately we haven't got a phone."

He wasn't sure whether she was a foreigner or not. But she must have some sort of problem in understanding. Torsten felt his decisiveness crumbling:

"There's an old guy nearby called Petterson. He's very helpful. He's actually lent us a wheelbarrow and a couple of shovels. I should think he'd probably let you use his telephone too if my friend comes along and talks to him."

While he was speaking – and it was without doubt an unusually long speech to have come from Torsten – he was examining the woman's face. This was hardly the face of someone who was after his wallet. It was a large, open face. Her pale blue eyes looked into his with a certain steadiness. One of them was surrounded by dark and rather yellowish shadows. Had she walked into an open door in the dark, or had someone struck her? It was actually the face of a strong person, a little too broad, very open, and yet somehow help-less. In some way those cool blue eyes were tired. It was as if they'd seen the worst. And right now it was him they were studying.

For the moment he felt himself rather at the mercy of this inspection. He didn't really mind. It was so seldom that any-one took a proper look at him that he couldn't remember when it had happened last. He ran his hand over the stubble of his beard. There hadn't been any time to shave this morning; just a little cold water on his face. And perhaps not the day before either. Yesterday was so far back in time that he had no idea what had happened then. And now this visitor had come just when he was getting back to the wall again. My wall, the only wall I've done for a very long time. The only thing that's given this wretched day any meaning.

And now it would most likely never be finished, of course.

"It's shameful to say, but he's locked me and the children out, and is refusing to let us in again. The only thing that will help is if I can speak to him. It's no good standing knocking at the door. That's why I need a telephone."

Torsten paused for quite a while, in fact so long that the smaller child started to scream, which didn't make the conversation any easier. If only bloody Stiggsy would come out and give him a helping hand.

She couldn't really be foreign after all. The fact that she was so slow on the uptake might just be because she was so exhausted. Perhaps she hadn't slept for a long time?

"I don't know," said Torsten hesitantly. "If things are as bad as that, perhaps it would be better to phone the *authorities* somewhere?"

The woman gave a short, sharp, joyless laugh. Torsten bit his lip. As soon as he said it he realised it wasn't very good advice. And no better for coming from him. He himself would rather starve to death, put barbed wire on top of the fence at home and let hungry Alsatians loose in what was left of his garden, than let in any damned authorities. He remembered with a shudder of discomfort how it had been a year or two back when there was a census. She shook her head and went towards the door, but without taking the children with her. They were both sitting on the floor and bawling their heads off now. Stig, who must have been up there after all messing about with that strange safe, was coming down the stairs – with rather slow and faltering steps, it seemed. He was noticeably pale. He surely couldn't have strained himself on that damned safe?

He doesn't look at all well, Torsten thought. There's definitely something wrong with him, but I can't quite make out what. He was holding his head as if he had a pain in it. Or maybe it was simply that he couldn't believe his own eyes when he saw this great big woman and her children.

"How are you feeling, then?" Torsten asked.

"Not very good. I felt a bit odd for a while. But it's better now."

"I said you shouldn't keep on trying to shake that damned safe. It's just stupid."

"Who's she? What are these children? What does she want?"

"To use the phone. But we haven't got one. She's been locked out." He was looking at the smaller child absentmindedly while it went on screaming so loudly that it hurt his ears.

"Poor little devil! It must be hard for babies! They don't have any swearwords they can use."

The child stopped as if it had actually thought of something, and suddenly smiled a radiant smile. But Stiggsy had no eyes for the child right now. He went on with his own train of thought as if he had difficulty getting away from it just at that moment.

"You know, this house is an evil house. I'm discovering weird new things all the time. Nasty things! God alone knows whether we'll get out of it alive. And what are all these children doing here now? And why should this woman want to use the telephone? Hasn't she got one of her own?"

And with another glance at the children – the little boy was

84

still hiding behind his mother and just peeping out from time to time – he added:

"Perhaps they're hungry?"

"There's nothing left to eat here. Nor to drink, either, for that matter. For some strange reason," Torsten answered.

Meanwhile with a sudden movement the woman disappeared out into the entrance-hall. She literally dragged the boy out by the hand.

"Hell, we can't have that! This won't bloody do! We can't leave her like that! Can't I at least run out and see which way she went?"

"OK," said Torsten. "I'm staying here. You go off out and look after her. Or is it better if we do it the other way round?"

"No, for God's sake. If I can only catch up with her."

"Well – just take it easy."

"Will we ever get this damned tiling finished?"

"I'm beginning to wonder. Go on! Otherwise you'll never catch her up."

The man with the goldfish

S HE TOOK her children and went. As she left she was
muttering dark threats about people who squat in other
people's houses, about old drunks and offending public
decency, and about having a good mind to tell someone what
was going on over there. The strange characters there were,
renovating houses nowadays! And she had no idea where to
go now. With the baby on her arm she stood indecisively by
the hedge. The little boy threw a last glance back towards the
house. The funny old men had been interesting. He'd never
seen anything quite like it before. He would have liked to
stop and play with Stig. He was lagging so much that his
mother told him off; he looked round eagerly after Stig, but
went along anyway. He was someone who'd learned the rules.

She didn't know whether to go back or to carry on up the
street. The longer she was away, the angrier he would get.
But if she went back he wouldn't open up, and would humili-
ate her again in front of the neighbours (dreadful neighbours
with cold, inquisitive eyes) by making her stand outside banging on the door. Perhaps the baby would start screaming
again? Would they threaten to call the police as they had
before? The police would mean the danger of the children
being taken away from her, into care. She might never see

them again. These neighbours were capable of that, it was obvious. Hadn't that big bastard opposite already yelled "keep your children in order, you bloody foreigners". She wasn't a foreigner at all. She came from Tornedalen, up in the north, and so looked a bit foreign and dark, but it wouldn't do any good to explain. Was everyone who wasn't born on these desolate clay plains of Uppland a bloody foreigner? What was it that was so special about belonging to this region, for God's sake?

Phoning: what good would that do? She might just as well walk away from it all, jump in the river, into the ice-cold water and feel it close over her head. But she wasn't even sure whether that would make him regret anything. All doors were closed; not even the path of death was open to her. It was just something dark that looked promising simply because you didn't know what it contained. She too was someone who had learned the rules.

He had no trouble catching up with her. She was walking at a slow but resolute pace, leaning into the wind, which now had turned very cold. Although she was a tall woman, she seemed to have short legs. She was almost dragging the little boy along with her. And Stig had a feeling that he'd never seen such a hopeless person – so totally without hope – in his whole life. Where did all the hopelessness come from?

It seemed to him for a moment as if hopelessness was the only thing that human beings really had in common. Everything else was temporary and could disappear at any time.

"OK," said Stig. "Where are you going now? Are you going home or going away?"

"I don't know any more," the woman said.

"What's your name?" Stig asked.

"Seija. If it matters."

"Torsten and I agreed that I should try to come along and help you. Talk your husband round, so to speak. You can't go about like this with little children. It's autumn now and so damned cold and miserable on the streets. They'll catch a chill."

"I'm not so sure you'd manage it. You look rather old and scruffy. I wonder if it wouldn't be better if you minded your own business. What are you actually up to in that house?"

"Well, if only I knew. The job's not mine. It's his. Torsten Bergman's. I've known him for years and went along with him for a while because it's so boring sitting at home. I don't think he quite knows either what it is we're doing. Tiles have to be put up in a bathroom. That's what's got to be done. And that's what we're up to. And in a kitchen, it seems. But the odd thing is that neither my friend nor I have seen a single person all day. I don't know whether I'm so keen on the job any more. The house is strange in some way. And no one coming to tell us what we have to do, either. We've had to work it out for ourselves. Are we going the right way now? Are we going home to your place, to talk some sense into that husband of yours?"

"We're not going anywhere at the moment. You can see the boy doesn't want to walk. He's too tired."

"Shall I put him on my shoulders? Do you want to sit on my shoulders? Up you go. You can see everything much better from up there. There we are. That's right."

For Stig that wasn't as easy as it might seem. He'd never had any children, since his wives always tended to leave him before it was time to start thinking about such hazardous undertakings. And actually he couldn't remember really having had anything to do with children since he himself was a child.

And the only memories he had of them were that they'd fought him. Outside the old factory-workers' houses in Hallstahammar, in the school playground, everywhere – there had been constant fighting and scratching, about a ball, about a dead sparrow they'd found, about anything and everything. Nor had he ever thought of himself as a child. He had the feeling that he'd gone direct from birth to secondary school (which he remembered as chalk dust, the master's massive nose-blowing into a gaudy handkerchief, and exciting colour pictures published by Norstedt & Sons of stone-age people and medieval knights. They were obviously the kind of things that were done at school. And then there was the apprentice-ship at the Bulten factory, an abominable place where the noise itself scared him. Older workmates played silly jokes on apprentices, like sending them to the foreman to get a rule of thumb and other stupid things).

Now he was standing here on the street, tired and wretched and with a not insignificant headache (one of the kind that throbs in your head in time with your pulse) and didn't know where he was going or how he should deal with the problem that had been entrusted to him out of the blue. And yet he was glad to have it.

To his utmost astonishment the boy was as good as gold about getting up on his shoulders, so good in fact that Stig almost had the impression that he liked him.

Strange products of nature with their seeds that grow, their leaves that unfold with the same blind hopefulness whether they've landed in a crack in the asphalt of a motorway or in a garden bed. Isn't there something terrible in that? Or does it perhaps have to be so? If people could decide for them-selves where and when they should be born, perhaps no people would be born at all? Life doesn't seem to serve our purposes, that much is obvious. We take it as we find it and make of it what we can. But the fact that we exist, that we are here, happens long before we know what to do with it. That's the whole problem: that we haven't asked for it. And then have to think of something to do with it.

Shall we go for a little ride, then?

With some difficulty, he set off. One thing was clear: his headache didn't improve with the fresh air. He suddenly had a distinct memory (which went straight through the headache and shone like a very small sun) of how it had been to sit on his own father's shoulders. To be able to see things. God knows what. Perhaps a brass band marching down the road to the factory? And that safe feeling that every little boy had his own father and was sitting on his father's shoulders. That's how things were in the world, as a matter of course.

Riding on his father's shoulders meant brass bands, circus parades, fire-eaters and huge flags flapping in the wind on May Day. And somehow it also meant fresh waffles with sugar on. What a shame that he didn't have any waffles to give the boy! Then Stig got short of breath again and had to put him down. But Seija had set off walking again, with her peculiarly short steps. Towards home, he assumed. The boy smelled of little boy, and it seemed likely that he hadn't changed his jersey for quite a few days. His shoes were split – they were canvas shoes – but at least the laces were well and truly tied. Stig could certainly never have untied them if he'd had to.

The question was simply how he should act in these circumstances, which he hadn't asked for. Would he be let in? And if he was let in to this man, who was obviously cruel enough to lock out his own flesh and blood like this – was that actually what he wanted?

In fact, the problem wasn't what he might meet there, but that he would have to leave them there.

And with a sudden shift of thought that's typical of people who don't know which way to turn, he began to worry about that damned leak in the house. Was Torsten having to stop and scoop water out now, while Stig was held up here, or was he able to carry on working on his tiles again for a while?

"Do you think we should ring him up first?" Stig asked after a hundred yards or so.

The fact that the boy was being good didn't stop him making Stig's headache considerably worse.

"Shall we try ringing up and talking sense into him? So that he lets us in?"

"You can do what you like," she said.

It sounded rather as if she no longer had very much to do with the matter.

There was a telephone box down at the corner. She said you could see the house now, over there between the trees. It looked a really nice building, a housing association block from the fifties or thereabouts. A time when there was still a little more quality in house-building. Obviously they must have had a bit of money, at least at some time. Getting a flat in blocks like that wasn't cheap nowadays.

You can do what you like – that's easily said. But the telephone box had been vandalised, of course, the flex cut, and some kind of disgusting ketchup smeared over the handset: it was exactly what could have been expected. What strange kind of people could they be who went round cutting off the wires on public telephones? Stig couldn't remember having seen anything like that in his youth. Never in Hallsta nor during the cold winters of the war years in the little town of Malmköping. Who could want to do such harm to others? Were there people who really wanted it to be so inhuman and desolate out on the streets?

And there was probably no point in going to that chap Petterson. They'd already passed his house and it didn't look as if the old man was at home. He'd been kind enough before and lent them tools and things. The question was whether he'd turn out to be so kind if Stig thrust himself on him with a whole family. There has to be a limit on how much you can demand of others.

Just before the corner of the street there was a sort of bakery and café, with nobody at the tables and a miserable lady behind the counter. The doorbell rang as he went in and Stig bent low enough for the little boy not to bang his head. There was a smell of bread in the air, something that many people like to associate with goodness. But the old dear behind the counter was not a particularly good person.

No sooner had Stig expressed his modest wish to use the phone – for a local call, of course – than she pointed to the door with her evil, bony finger. Like the witch in the fairy-tale! And she even had the nerve, this infernal old woman, to say something about the police. Well, he'd certainly got out of an empty and frightening house and into the real world again, but the devil alone knew whether it was very much better!

Stig went slowly back towards the door, wavering between his new-found pride in the fact that the little fellow actually liked him and was enjoying sitting on his shoulders, and the heightened irritability of his substantial hangover.

He realised full well the difficulty of holding on to a little boy's feet to stop him falling and hurting himself, while simultaneously throttling a repulsive, mean and unfriendly old hag of a café owner, an undertaking which would indubitably need both hands. So, displaying a sudden affection towards the little boy sitting so well-behaved and trustingly on his shoulders (people can harbour very good and very evil feelings at the same time: that's something that the bloody priests have never reckoned with, but that's the way it is), Stig had to content himself with turning round and saying (admittedly in a rather loud voice):

"You repulsive old cow, watch yourself. I can tell you that both you and your arthritic old finger will soon be lying in the grave and rotting. And then it'll be too late to regret all the unkindness you've shown. Towards the smallest of your brothers. Remember that when the worms are eating you!"

Whether the old crone turned pale or not was not easy to tell, because Stig was already outside the door that he slammed behind him. That didn't matter too much. But deep in his soul Stig had the warm feeling of satisfaction that sometimes comes from knowing you've uttered a powerful curse and that it's really hit home. Stig was surprisingly good at things like that. In his boyhood he had often managed to throw a snowball over his shoulder on the way to school and hit some tormentor right in the eye. Stig had never seen anything unusual in that: it had always just been part of his natural abilities.

The boy on his shoulders burst out laughing. A real open, happy little laugh that came with the same suddenness as icicles falling down a drainpipe on a sunny March day and running out on the pavement. The laugh made Stig very happy.

"To hell with the phone," he said to the woman, who was standing pale and expectant on the pavement. She hadn't gone into the café and hadn't much idea of what had happened. But for a moment the shadow on her face was dissolved by the little boy's laugh.

From that moment the whole walk was slightly changed. And immediately so much easier to go on with.

The story he later told Torsten was roughly as follows:

"They live in a housing-association block down at the corner. One of those old three-storey buildings from the forties. Really smart and nice. So we tramp up the stairs, her first and me following. And I really begin to wonder what I'm doing there.

"I'm not as strong as I was, you see. And half a day with your bloody wall tiling has an effect on my heart these days, that's for certain. I'm not really made for leaping up stairs any longer. I was behind from the start, I heard her ring the doorbell up above, I heard the door open, and when I finally got up there, out-of-breath and feeling terrible, the door's ajar.

"I go in and there he is sitting reading a book. In the middle of the afternoon. And by the armchair there's a big aquarium of goldfish, the biggest and nicest looking goldfish I've ever seen. It must have been a two-roomed flat but I didn't see more than the room he sat in. And I must say that apart from the aquarium it wasn't a particularly tidy room. Newspapers in piles on the floor, children's toys lying all over the place where they'd happened to land. It's quite horrifying the amount of untidiness some people can put up with.

"His wife is standing there and obviously can't think of anything to say right then, and her husband is sitting there in his comfortable armchair and has nothing to say either. By

94

that stage I was so exhausted from the stairs that I'd have liked to take over the armchair. Hard to say how old he is, maybe forty, or younger. Well, the problems here seem to be solved, so I can't think what the hell I'm supposed to be doing there.

"'They're very fine goldfish,' I say.

"'Thanks very much: I spent a lot on them,' he says.

"Then there's silence again. So I try once more and say that it's a pity you can't have other fish together with goldfish. The gills give off so much ammonia that other fish can't tolerate it. He looks at me as if he's only just noticed that I'm in the room.

"'That's no problem,' he says. 'Why should you want other fish?'

"'It probably gets very tedious,' I say. 'Always seeing the same fish swimming backwards and forwards. I'd really get tired of it if I had to sit watching goldfish all the time. They're all the same colour.'

"'Not at all,' he says. 'They've got masses of colours if you look carefully. It's different with every movement. Who are you anyway? What are you doing here?'

"'I came to help your wife get in. You'd locked her and the kids out. If you want the truth, what happened was that Seija, your wife, came and said that you'd thrown her and the children out and locked them out. Is that the way to treat your wife and children? Shouldn't we be happy with our children for as long as we have them?'

"'Well, perhaps not exactly *thrown out*,' Seija quickly corrected, 'I said *locked out*.'

"'Well, otherwise I'd hardly be here, would I?'

"'He didn't throw us out. He locked us out.'

"'I didn't at all. It was the door that blew shut. It's not easy for me to keep a check on whether the door is open or closed.

You can hear she's slandering me. That's all she does all the time. She always wants to make rows and attract attention. Otherwise she thinks life isn't interesting. If she doesn't watch out, the children will probably be taken into care by the local authority soon. You're probably the sort that would go running round and squealing to the authorities.'

" 'No,' I say. 'I'm not that sort.'

" 'You sound damned stuck-up to me. Are you sure you aren't connected with the authorities in some *tiny* way?'

" 'Of course I'm sure,' I say, 'but there are limits to how far you can go just to get some peace from your wife and children and sit watching goldfish. There's a bit more than goldfish in the world. We have a little responsibility for those we've brought into the world, haven't we?'

"If he hasn't already jumped up and hit me on the chin by this point, then at least he'll do so now, I think to myself, so I get rid of the screwdriver (that I had with me in my back pocket) and put it on the table so that at least no one will injure himself on that. But he, the crazy devil, just stays sitting in his chair and puts his head in his hands. And to tell the truth, I think he's crying.

"I must say it's terribly embarrassing. I, an old man of seventy, have never seen a bloke cry before. Then he pulls himself together and is able to speak again and says something like:

" 'I just want to be left in peace for a while.'

" 'Well, who the hell doesn't want a bit of peace,' I say. 'But you don't get it just because you want it. And by the way, there's something odd here. I almost don't believe it. I think I recognise you.'

" 'What?' he says, taken aback. 'I thought I recognised you, too. But I can't for the life of me remember where from.'

"'You're Alf,' I say. 'Or Alfred, to be exact. You're my aunt's youngest boy.'"

How it all ended and how he took his leave of these strange people was something he didn't want to go on to tell.

The day resists intrusion

TORSTEN BERGMAN went on working furiously. Back
at the house. What else could he do? He was banging
about and sweating, he was dipping the trowel into the bucket
of tile cement and spreading it over the rough walls, pressing
the tiles on with the utmost precision and tightening the cord
from time to time. You could see already that when the grouting was done it would all be pretty good. It would look expensive and stylish. And presumably that was what was expected
of him? Plain and dark blue and stylish. Obviously there were
a couple of Poggenpohl taps missing – but there'd be no
problem in replacing them. You shouldn't dwell on details
when it was the overall concept that mattered. And though
the water was starting to cover the floor again, it was slower
now that Torsten had plugged the tap connectors with bits
of wood. In short, he was once again master of the situation.

He knew no more than before who he was working for, or
why, or for what money. The way he felt now, it wasn't so
important. He was working, some of the time happy and
sometimes hissing with fury when things went wrong. But he
was working. And the time was beginning to be filled with
meaning despite everything.

They hadn't been there long. And yet the little children
had left a feeling of emptiness behind them. Not their voices,
not the way they looked, but just a peculiar wordless warmth

that they left behind in the room. He was very concerned about how it would turn out. He could only hope that Stiggsy would be man enough to handle it. But there wasn't much to him really, he'd looked so pale and weak and wretched by the time he went. It was no joke that he'd drunk most of the aquavit: a damned sight more than one bottle out of the three they'd bought.

It was really amazing how some people could drink.

And he'd paid for that out of his advance from the Poggen-pohl taps! That was a fine thing. Torsten groped in the breast pocket of his old torn leather jacket for the paper he'd written everything down on. He'd have to be able to account for it eventually. He had a very distinct memory of having stuffed it in his breast pocket (the last time was when he'd shown it to Stig). And here was a crumpled piece of paper, just as expected. But it wasn't the same one. This was a different one: a note on a torn-off piece of the slightly stiff card cover of the telephone book that he'd made in the morning of that self-same long day when he'd felt so sleepy and dreadful. Half distractedly he read what he'd written and stuffed the scrap of paper, that now completely unimportant scrap of paper, back in his pocket again. But the damned paper with his financial reckonings on he had most probably put in the glove box of the car. And he had neither the time nor the inclination to go out looking for it now. So he'd just have to leave it. If the worst came to the worst he could write it all out again. Truth to tell, he had an excellent memory.

Despite all the glasses and bottles, it must be said.

When Torsten was a little boy – much too small to have any idea what it was all about – he had been a teetotaller. He used to go with his mother, redeemed and Free Church as she was, to temperance meetings, where eloquent gentlemen from distant Västerås or even more distant Örebro would talk about the dangers of insobriety. You could get cirrhosis of the liver. (One speaker even had a shrivelled-up liver with him and showed it to the audience. He didn't say where he'd got it from, which had made Torsten suspicious. Besides, at that time Torsten thought that all internal organs always looked very strange.) The audience consisted entirely of very sober people, mostly elderly women, so the speakers must have felt very successful in their efforts. Cirrhosis of the liver wasn't the only danger from insobriety. There was always a risk that Parliament would be taken over by drunks who had no idea how Sweden should be governed. And anyone could see that that would be to the country's detriment in times of trouble. So they had to make sure that sober liberals got into Parliament and not drunken socialists who might get up to anything. (Torsten Bergman had retained his distaste for socialists all his life, but unfortunately it seemed as if they had become more and more sober and effective over the years.)

For as long as Torsten could remember, his Aunt Svea, who was the cold-buffet manageress at the Grand Hotel in Stockholm (a place that was posher, but for that very reason also more sinful, than others), had told the most terrible stories of what drunkenness could lead to. Drunkards would sit in restaurants and lose the ability to keep themselves in order. Hadn't her friend Charlie, who was a porter at the same establishment, once had to help a gentleman who had dropped his braces in the lavatory and then nonchalantly pulled the shitty braces over his clean and elegant dinner shirt, to make his way discreetly to a car, and been given fifty crowns for his trouble? Weren't there farmers who had drunk so much they'd had to give up their farms and land? Sat and drunk in hotels while their children didn't even have a loaf of bread. (Torsten often thought it strange that Aunt Svea could actually allow herself to work in such a place that only brought about misery, but 'cold-buffet manageress' sounded reassuring. It gave the impression that she at least didn't allow herself to be dragged into these fearful goings-on. Hot-buffet manageress would have been worse.)

In fact you could divide the whole of humanity into two groups, the good and the bad. At one stage of his life when he was about seventeen and had been a newspaper boy on the Örebro–Västerås train, he'd begun to realise the awful truth: that the adherents of temperance weren't actually in the majority at all, despite what he'd always believed.

"PAPERS AND BOOKS!"

His job was to walk up and down through the carriages with a great heavy bag right through the whole long journey. The evening papers came aboard in Hallsberg, and the previous paperboy, a pale and pimply youth, very tall and with a sickly appearance, would hand over to him. They had to check their accounts before the train set off again and the other one jumped off. The station foreman, a huge man, had no patience with newspaper boys who delayed the train. In fact he probably regarded paperboys in general as an evil.

The bag hurt your back like the devil, particularly at the beginning of the journey, and when the express leaned over on the bends you had to be careful not to fall on to the passengers. It happened a lot when you started, and was not always taken in good part. But sometimes it was, even with coarse laughter when he landed on the lap of some fat and not always unwilling lady who would hold on to him with her hands clasped round his waist and pretend that she'd found the sweetheart she'd been searching for. No. It wasn't good for Torsten's self-confidence. Here, standing in the dust and smell of damp plaster, nearly fifty years later, he could still turn bright pink when painful memories like that came to mind.

"PAPERS AND BOOKS!"

It used to get better nearer to Västerås. There weren't many who used to buy books. And it was only rubbish: detective stories and suchlike trash. But the newspapers sold well. When times were uncertain and dangerous they really went like hot cakes. The bag soon got lighter and it was easier and easier to get through the carriages. The day that blessed Ivar Kreuger shot himself in Paris was a really wonderful day. His bag was empty of newspapers half way down the train.

He could actually feel in his back when he got home to Hallstahammar whether it had been a good day or a bad day in the Great Depression. The worse the day for humanity, the better it was for Torsten's back, he used to say to himself.

Nevertheless: on these trains with all their fat gentlemen in first class and serious farmers, high-spirited rustic conscripts and comparatively decent girls in third class, it was easy to see that it was the disorderly and intemperate people who were in the majority out there in the world, not, as at home where his mother lived in Hallstahammar, the sober and the religious.

Here there were farmers drinking slyly from whole bottles and half bottles behind their newspapers, afraid of being seen by the ticket collector. Here there were youths clinking beer bottles in plain carrier bags. And in the restaurant car everyone was doing it happily and joyfully without any slyness at all. If you imagined that this was a normal example of the lives of these disorderly people that you were seeing here on the train, then it was simply appalling. But there didn't seem to be any speaker wanting to come and lecture to them. And they vomited and misbehaved, worst of all when they were called up to their regiments.

He could simply never bring himself to talk about the misery he'd seen when he came home to his mother. And anyway she was usually asleep when he got in, tired and wretched from her scrubbing and cleaning at the bank.

Because of all this, because of this childhood and youth full of temperance and free of sin, Torsten Bergman had always had a deep aversion to every form of excess and disorder. The same aversion that he felt now when he couldn't find the slip of paper with his accounts on about the advance for materials he had collected that same morning.

When he had finally tasted alcohol – and that was with his friends in the Royal Upland Regiment when he was doing his National Service – it was *an entirely different matter*. When the first intoxication after a few swigs out of the communally-purchased bottle had risen through his pimply and immature body, he'd felt a very clear sensation of having found a homeland. He could never have imagined that anything so wonderful actually existed! It was, it seemed to him, as if you'd lived all your life in a little one-roomed flat and one day discovered that there was a huge room (light and welcoming, with big windows in all four walls, and billowing curtains and birdsong outside) hidden behind a wallpapered door.

But *that* couldn't have anything to do with the other thing, that low and ruinous activity that the temperance speakers warned against? Anybody could see that this was something good, this was like coming home to yourself. When he'd finished his National Service he'd started drinking quite heavily, or as heavily as his circumstances allowed, and they were quite modest. But in his heart and soul he'd always remained a teetotaller.

Drunkenness was a form of worthlessness and disorder. But above all it was something that others fell into.

He himself used aquavit to achieve an order of a higher kind. An inner feeling of the meaningfulness of the world, you could perhaps say. For years he'd found it hard to get any sensible work done at all if he didn't have a few swigs at lunchtime or just after, but at the time he detested his friends drinking on the job. That was self-contradictory, of course, and he realised it. But he had a strong feeling that the world had to be contradictory to be able to function. That was quite simply the way it was created. And no other world than that was imaginable, with all its contradictions.

You could perhaps say that there was a constant battle going on in Torsten between order and disorder, where disorder nearly always won, yet where the hope for order remained. This orderliness made him go out to the car now and open the glove box. And just as he'd expected, there was the piece of paper with his accounts on it, a bit crumpled but exactly as he'd put it there:

Credit:	1230.00
Two returned taps, Poggenpohl brand	
(Uppsala Builders' Merchants)	

Debit:	
Tile cement, Väärtilä, 4 tubs @ 35.90	143.60
4 tubs grey grouting @ 24.90	99.60
Various tools and equipment	470.00
To be repaid to contractor	516.80

He went back into the house irritated by the feeling that there was still something that had escaped his notice. As he angrily poured more water into the bucket and stirred the remains of the tile cement (he was really hoping that it would last until the end of the day), he stuck his glasses in his jacket pocket again and immediately discovered the other piece of paper, the one with the address on. He put his glasses on again, read it, shook his head and stuffed it back into his pocket.

The thing about messages is that there aren't many we actually want. Most of them we're better off without. Muttering to himself and shaking his head, he returned to his wall. It was time to break open the metal bands on a new bundle of tiles. His hand holding the pliers was trembling a little.

Why had he gone in for photography so much as a boy? Was it his pleasure in the mysterious, the picture that emerged from the developing liquid? Or the delighted and slightly anxious comments of relations and girls and the old women at the chapel when they saw themselves in the photographs?

Or was it the fact that you could hold on to a picture? And sort of fish it back up out of time, that sluggish brown river of pictures and voices that disappeared?

There were unpleasant pictures too, of course. A lorry full of cement pipes had once been hit by a train on the level crossing at Tomtebo. The driver, the poor guy, had escaped (at least that's how he remembered it), but the great heavy Scania-Vabis lorry had been completely wrecked. He'd arrived on his bike, both fascinated and frightened, and had photographed the poor wrecked lorry and its broken and scattered pipes. From all different angles. Right until the fire brigade came and cleared up the whole mess. What was it he actually wanted to capture on that expensive plate film? His own wretchedness? The loss of his father? A cargo in transit that would never reach its destination?

Midges in the brain? There are actually thoughts that can get into your head as if they were some kind of insect, persistent, piercing, parasitical.

This piece of paper in his pocket was a thought like that. He didn't want to think about it, and yet it stubbornly insisted on coming back. All the time.

It's a bit like when you've got a blister in your mouth and your tongue keeps on and on going there. It doesn't do any good, and yet your damned tongue keeps going to it. It can't leave it alone.

So he had another look at the paper with the address on. And there was no denying what was written on it. That piece of paper held a secret that he didn't want to acknowledge.

And how in hell's name anyone could confuse Malmwood Road with Woodland Road – surely that was something completely beyond any human comprehension?

A man without real morality

N O ONE ASKED S TIG to sit down, so he just remained standing in the doorway. That was probably best, because his trousers must have been pretty dusty after several hours in that far from homely house. It wasn't much more homely here: everything looked rather improvised, to put it mildly. Though at least there was a young relation of his here, and children complaining in the kitchen, and the clinking of china being washed up.

"There's a lot that's not very easy to talk about," said Alf. "To start with, I'd like to point out that I'd rather not be called Alf. No one's called me Alf since I was a boy. My name's Alfred."

"I'm very sorry, I couldn't have known that."

"OK. I'll let you off. The goldfish, on the other hand, are only a start. They're totally new for me, too. I've just come out of prison, you see. Only a couple of months ago. But it feels as if it was only the other day. That's why I don't much want to go out. And like sitting at home here in peace. That's why doors slam closed. Wives go out with children."

"What a helluva thing to happen," said Stig. "Prison, that's a bit much."

"Well, you'd think so. But that's how things go."

"It can't really have been a minor thing, either, if you got prison for it?"

Seija was standing in the kitchen doorway, with the baby still on her arm.

"Don't talk to him about it. He just gets miserable if you ask him that sort of thing. He feels ill if he starts thinking about it."

"Not at all. I don't mind talking about it. I've got nothing to be ashamed of."

"I don't think anyone in the family has heard from you for years. There aren't that many left, either. I guess I must be the oldest one now that Uncle Ragnar's died. I thought you lived in Johanneshov?"

"That was years ago."

"Weren't you doing oil paintings, too? Some kind of pictures?"

"Well, not any more."

"What happened to them, then?"

He shouted out to the kitchen: "Are you making coffee?"

Stig wondered how to continue the conversation. It had taken such a peculiar turn, he thought. It was a strange day, this, when all you did was bump into odd people. And all of them in some way connected with the past.

"I don't know whether you know this. But when I was at school I was very good at painting and drawing. A lot better than everyone else. I could draw an old brass decanter with reflections and sheen and everything so that the art mistress was beside herself with joy. I could draw a screwed-up piece of paper with every fold and every shadow in the right place. The teachers thought it was a bit uncanny. At the beginning they used to wonder whether I was actually cheating. But I wasn't.

"Well, my teacher wanted me to apply to the Academy. But it sort of didn't happen. My father wanted me at home in the workshop, though I'd probably have got away if I'd asserted myself. But it was the busy season just then."

"He used to repair lawn mowers and rotavators and things like that, didn't he?"

"Yes, and hired them out too. There was a lot to do for a few years. Then he dropped down dead one day and it was a bit too late for me to start studying. I did some painting, anyway. And even sold a few to two old ladies who kept an antique shop. They sold my efforts to their normal customers. There was quite a demand for a while. Of course, it wasn't really modern things that I did. Not, as they say, in the current fashion. Because I didn't understand it. But it wasn't junk art either. They were the sort of paintings you'd expect in a shop like that. Landscapes and things. Fine old Norrland landscapes."

"Was that in Johanneshov, then?"

"Hell, no, it was here in Rotebro. It was after my father died. I divided my time between repairing old furniture and painting."

"Well, well. I like landscapes myself."

"Anyway, one day some characters turned up and asked if I could paint something for them. A commission. So to speak. They wanted a Norrland landscape. By Helmer Osslund. But Osslund's paintings had got so expensive now. So I took the train into Stockholm and had a look at Osslund. At the Modern Art Museum. He was good. And not particularly difficult. I told them: 'OK, you can have an Osslund, but I'll want twenty thousand crowns for it. And ten thousand in advance for material and things.' Well, I enjoyed it. I've never been up to Norrland, but by that time I'd painted so many Norrland landscapes that I knew exactly how things looked up there. Blue shadows against white snow. Shadows are always in complementary colours, you know. And violet-hued dwarf birch trees that would soon be coming into leaf in May.

Well, these guys came again and paid up as arranged. And wanted a couple more. But I don't think I signed them Helmer Osslund. I didn't. A thing like that would never occur to me. I can't imagine going in for that kind of dishonesty, you see."

"No. But presumably someone else did?"

"Possibly. I don't know. I didn't get involved. Anyway, isn't painting something always a kind of forgery? Isn't it? You paint a tree. That's OK. But you haven't made the tree. You've only pretended that you've made a tree. Perhaps the tree itself is only a trick, a representation of something else? How can you know that it isn't?"

"I've never really thought about it!"

"No. But that's the way it is.

"Now some guy comes along and does a mountain birch that Helmer Osslund has already done better some time in the twenties. It's a copy of a copy of a birch, right? So what you then have to ask yourself is why it should be so particularly bad or evil to copy something that's already been copied. It's already been copied once. It's fiction and lies from the start, so what difference does it make? I can paint a chair. But why the devil can't I make a chair? Wouldn't it be a lot better to be able to make chairs?"

"But it's not so well paid – right?"

"Yes, I got paid more and more by those two guys. I suspect they did all right out of me. But a lot came my way too. They asked whether I wouldn't like to have a bit bigger advance so that I could buy a housing-association flat, and I was pretty keen . . . So I moved to Uppsala with my wife and our first child. Yes, it's this flat that I paid for from that.

"How's the coffee coming on, by the way? No? Ah, well. We'll have to do without, then.

"Then they came and asked whether I could do something

in the style of Carl Kylberg. West-coast landscape, a lot of colour, a bit fuzzy. OK, I said. Show me how Kylberg paints, and I'll see. So I spent a few more days in the museum. And the Kylbergs were a real success. I had to give up almost everything else I was doing. A bit of insurance I was selling, and so on. I was quite simply better at painting like Kylberg than like Osslund, and I did masses of west-coast landscapes, till I began to know the west coast as well as I did Norrland. Though I'd never been there, either. I started to feel really well-travelled.

"The Kylbergs went like hot cakes, and so I told these guys that I needed a car. Of course you must have a car, they said, but not just any old heap. We'll fix you up with a good car. So one day they come driving up with a one-year-old Mercedes, leather trim and cassette deck and speakers and everything. You can imagine that Seija and the kid – I had just the one boy at that time – were pretty excited. Not to mention how envious the neighbours were. We went on long trips on Sundays to Skokloster and Kvicksund and I don't know where. Yes, some Sundays we even went as far as the big restaurant at Kolbäck.

"I think it was the car that made the neighbours really angry. Anyway, it was about that time that they began to complain about the smell of turpentine. I've never minded turpentine. I like all the chemicals you use for oil painting, from turpentine and thinner, to varnish and beeswax. But the neighbours started to claim that the smell of turpentine gave them allergies. They said that their children and the old folks were having to go to the doctor. And you shouldn't have a workshop at home in modern blocks. Oh, no. You had to have special permission from the local authority for that."

"But you're not going to tell me you ended up in prison for having a painter's studio at home in your flat?"

"Yes, I should be out in a shop! But let me tell you it all first. I can't break off in the middle. Not now I've started telling the whole story. Well, anyway, I began to realise that I wasn't exactly popular in the block. One morning someone had made a long scratch in the paint on my fine new car. Another morning the radio aerial was gone. So what did I do? I went over to acrylic, of course. Acrylic hardly smells at all. You mix acrylic with water. But acrylic is never the same. That's obvious. There's never the same subtlety. But obviously if you want to paint like Kylberg and lay the colour on thick, then acrylic is quite good. So I slung out the turpentine to please the damned neighbours and set to work with acrylic. At least it has the advantage of everything drying very fast. You speed up production, so to speak. Well, I carried on with my business and everything was fine and dandy for a few months and I was just starting to think about whether I shouldn't take a holiday in Majorca – I'd never been to Majorca either, not even in my painting, and I thought I could just do with a little holiday in April that year. Then one of these fellows rings up – Sixten and Uffe are their names – and is beside himself with rage. 'It's a catastrophe,' he says. I'm a joker and they should really set a heavy on me. 'What are you on about?' I say. 'What do you mean, catastrophe?' 'You've been painting in *acrylic*,' says Sixten. 'Of course it's bloody catastrophic.' 'The neighbours don't like the smell of turpentine,' I say. 'Carl Kylberg never painted in acrylic!' 'No, and thank the devil for that,' say I. 'It hadn't been invented in his day.' 'No. But now they've discovered that it's acrylic. So now everything's finished.' 'But I've never pretended that I'm Carl Kylberg,' I say.

"'*Don't talk rubbish*, Alf,' says this so-called friend. 'You know very well what it's all about. There might be a police investigation into all this. They're already after us. Uffe's already been questioned.' 'Well, that's his affair,' I say. 'I haven't signed any of them Kylberg.'

" '*You can't imagine,*' this guy says, 'that it's your miserable amateur paintings we've been after. Don't you imagine that any court would be taken in by that.'

" 'But,' I say, 'if you can sell them as Kylbergs they can't be so damned bad.' 'But that's just what I can't do,' he says. 'I've told you, they've discovered they're just acrylic crap.'

" '*What the hell do you know about art?*' I ask. '*Lies are one thing.* Kylberg is genuine, and so am I.' "

"So you mean," Stig interrupted, scratching the back of his neck thoughtfully (there seemed to be dust all over his hair that he hadn't noticed before), "that you ended up in prison as a forger of paintings."

"Not at all. Bloody terrible that there isn't even a drop of coffee in the house. When we've got an uncle here and everything."

"Thanks, but don't go to any trouble for me. I only wanted to make sure that your wife and children got home all right. I must get back to my work. The guy I'm helping might start getting worried."

"You don't bloody well go to prison nowadays for forging paintings. No, it was just that the devils wanted the car back. They were adamant. 'The car's mine,' I said. So they send over a couple of heavies who simply tow the car away. Debt collection firms have heavies like that nowadays, you know. They didn't even break into it, and didn't do anything to the ignition, either. Just towed it away. But they shouldn't have done that. That car was the only thing I had left from three years of artistic work. I was proud of it. That wasn't false."

"So what did you do then?"

"I poked around looking for a tip-off from various used car dealers till I found one who knew something. He thought he knew who they'd sold it to. So off I went to this guy – he had a house in Enskede – and there was my Mercedes, just as expected. New number-plates and everything, but the same old locks. I unlock it, right in this guy's garage drive, and start backing my old car out to drive it home. Then the bugger goes and stands in the way."

"I see."

"Yes, so unfortunately I have to back into him. And he didn't come out of it too well."

"But it was a bit of a cheek. What had he done to you?"

"Nothing. But he was standing in the way. So he got a bit dented. And I went to prison. For grievous bodily harm."

"Well, well. You're like Stalin or Hitler. You drive over everyone who gets in your way."

"That's not the same at all. We're not talking about Hitler and Stalin now. I was just trying to get my rights."

"Your rights?"

Stiggsy would probably have continued, but he was suddenly overcome by a terrible tiredness. And there was an uncomfortable little twinge of pain round his heart. The only thing he wanted to do was to make his way back to Torsten, at a nice slow, careful pace, and ask him to drive him home. Perhaps he'd overdone things by helping him with this weird job? On his way out he couldn't help glancing into the kitchen. Seija, Alf's wife, was feeding the little boy with rusks dipped in milk. He seemed to be very hungry and enjoying them immensely.

It's strange, thought Stig, what an appetite little children can have. And how quickly they learn the rules and still hope that everything will turn out all right.

In the long run, so to speak.

Work, for the night is coming

As a little Christian boy he had learned that despair was a sin, but it was questionable whether that teaching was any use to him now. In his wretched condition, Torsten was imagining that Sophie K. was a horrible old witch dressed in black who'd been there the whole time, invisible, just to obstruct him and keep him in the clutches of meaninglessness. He imagined her dressed in black and with intensely grey eyes. As grey as the water in a clay pit at Ekeby factory on a November day in the fifties. (A man had once drowned himself in a clay pit like that and he could still remember how unreal and grey and flaccid the corpse had looked when they pulled it out, shining with clay, in the dredging bucket.)

Human beings are complicated creatures. They have the ability, for example, literally not to see what they don't want to see. You meet a person in the street and don't recognise him. Because you don't want to see. The face reminds you of something you don't want to think of. Or it doesn't fit into what you want at the moment. In the fast-falling darkness of the winter evening Torsten Bergman was at least successful in one thing: he managed to suppress below the surface of his consciousness the realisation that he had worked meaninglessly all day long at the wrong address. The hidden knowledge was there and produced a kind of spurious energy in his hands and head, made him work hard and mechanically and swear a lot to himself and keep his eyes resolutely on his work. The only other thing he thought about was his glimpse of the little children who had been there. They reminded him so clearly of a happiness he must have known once upon a time and had now almost forgotten. A red thread running through the countless knots in the dirty grey rag mat of a day.

By now he was a long way from sense and reason and balance. He had a feeling of not belonging anywhere, of having nowhere to go, and that the only thing connecting him to the world was this bizarre, meaningless work. He looked around him with misty smarting eyes. (There was dust in his eyes and they were running as if he was crying.) These paltry few square yards of neatly-laid tiles were the only thing he owned. And he didn't even own them.

The evening had evidently arrived, there was still at least a square yard of wall to go, his shoes and socks were wet, and the tile cement wasn't as good or flexible as at the beginning. And the damned water was still splashing around his feet. However much he turned and twisted the pipe-wrench he could not get a proper grip on those bloody tap-connectors. It was as if they had a life of their own.

He couldn't see how he'd ever get the damned job finished at all. Not to mention the floor – that would really need re-tiling now as well.

He actually needed to stay here at least three or four more days. But there was no next day in this house, since it wasn't the right house. He wondered a lot about what they'd said in the other house, *the right house*, when he never turned up. They probably hadn't said much at all. Just rung for someone else and cursed the time they'd lost.

And how long had he been here? It felt like not one but

several days. He'd even lost count of the hours. A hunger that he couldn't do much about was gnawing at his stomach.

The door banged, as Torsten sat there like Job among the ashes, and in came Stiggsy. He looked a little pale and sat straight down with his back against the doorpost. He didn't even seem bothered whether he got wet or not.

"Well?" said Torsten.

"Mmm. It was a bit odd."

"But it went all right?"

"We were let in."

"How did they get on?"

"Strange people. I don't really understand them."

"How do you mean?"

"I mean I can't really grasp how people live nowadays. Or how their minds work, for that matter."

And Stiggsy told his story.

It didn't escape Torsten's notice that he stopped in the middle. It was obvious that there was something he didn't want to let out. But Torsten was too tired to press him. And besides, he himself had something that he wouldn't want to let on about for the world. So their secrets offset one another.

"He paints, too."

"Oh, what, his house?"

"No, not that sort. He paints pictures. But he doesn't think much of it. He thinks that paintings are just false."

"I see," said Torsten. "Well, he may be right."

"This wall we've done today is a real wall, anyway. It's a solid piece of work."

"Yes. I hope so," said Torsten, without any real conviction. "It was fun while it lasted, anyway. And thanks for all the help you gave me. I hope you didn't feel obliged to help me?"

"We always make up our own minds who we're going to help. When it comes down to it, that is."

"Yes. It must be time to go home now."

"Yes. You start getting your stuff together, so that I can sit quietly for a few minutes."

"Are you feeling bad?"

"No-o. Not really. But I'm a bit tired. And there's a pain in my chest. I'll just lie down for a while. With my jacket under my head, then it'll get better."

"I'll drive you home. No question about that. It's only up as far as Morgongåva. It won't take long. As you said: We always make up our own minds who we want to help."

"But I don't live in Morgongåva any more, I've told you. I live just nearby."

There was silence after that.

Torsten didn't quite know what to do next. But right at that moment there was a loud knocking at the door – no, more of a pounding than a knocking. It sounded as if by some strange coincidence the whole world had come to life again and was trying to get in.

"Who the hell can that be? It's half past eight!"

"You'll see, it'll be that Sophie out walking around again," said Torsten.

And for one brief moment he almost believed it himself.

New Directions Paperbooks—A Partial Listing

For complete listing request free catalog from
New Directions, 80 Eighth Avenue, New York 10011

†Bilingual

For complete listing request free catalog from
New Directions, 80 Eighth Avenue, New York 10011   †Bilingual